BRAIN-NATTER:
A Short Story Collection

By Adam McNelis

Published by Amazon KDP

Dedication

To the future, and all its boundless possibilities
…and jetpacks, I want a jetpack.

"Natter"

VERB

    informal

    Talk casually, especially on unimportant matters;
        'they nattered away for hours'

NOUN

    informal in singular

    A casual and leisurely conversation.
        'I could do with a drink and a natter'

CONTENTS

DRUNK, STUCK IN A LIFT, WITH STEVEN SPIELBERG

RED-G AND THE "NINJAS" IN THE WOODS

ELVIS AND THE MARS BAR

GLASGOW UNITED F.C

SNAKES AND LADDERS

DO ANDROIDS DREAM OF A 4-DAY WORKING WEEK?

ACOUSTIC VAMPIRE AT A PARTY

THE REAL MODERN SEXY CHRONICLES – PART 1: BLANK CANVAS BY THE BAR

THE REAL MODERN SEXY CHRONICLES – PART 2: WINGMEN OF THE WILD WEST

THE REAL MODERN SEXY CHRONICLES – PART 3: THE PLOOK

PIE HEAD

BILL SHAKESPEARE'S TIME TRAVELLING TEXT MESSAGE CONUNDRUM

THE LORD RETURNS

-

ARSEHOLE IN A HURRY: AN INTRODUCTION

For the longest time, rudderless, I'd dip my toe in this and that, getting nowhere, achieving nothing – an imposter at every turn.

This feeling, combined with an entire buffet of frustrating characteristics, like: the nervous energy that would fuel my non-stop gibbering; due to my inability to handle silence at parties, my knack of bringing up subjects completely random or wildly inappropriate, my being too thin-skinned; unable to differentiate between good hearted ribbing and authentic verbal assaults, my anorakish obsession with anything that peaked my interest, and my inconsistent skill-set when it came to picking up on social ques – stacked together, have often left me passive, numb almost, for large chunks of my life – with no mission in sight, I have simply sat back and watched the world fly by me.

But not now. Oh no no no. Now, I have been gifted with the realisation that what I feel are my flaws; my characteristics that have frustrated the life out of me, and that often disconnected me from those I sought to engage with the most, are the very same things that fuels THIS – my writing – and this is what irons out the creases of my thoughts and brings me clarity, and I am grateful that my frontal lobe was zapped with this epiphany in my thirties and not my eighties.

Still, every now and then I wish that I had realised all of this twenty years earlier – it would have saved a lot of heartache; because as bizarre as it may sound to some, the simple act of writing about what is on your mind seems to somehow manipulate reality, making the bruises, cuts, and scars that we inevitably gather along the way, just that little less painful.

In casual conversation, people are never shy in letting you know if you are a gas-bag, but an economy of words and a balanced noise-to-silence-ratio was never my jam – people just want you to get to the point – which is fair enough. But my natural inclination when face-to-face with someone was to always provide context; back-story, side-story, random facts, a beginning, a middle, and an end... then a prequel, a sequel, and the promise of regurgitating the same verbal spaghetti four beers later.

So rather than leaving a party or social gathering, and on the drive home doing the post-match-analyse-mental-beat-down about how all I did was talk mad random shit, my mind is at ease in that I now know I have explored all of this chaos and curiosity with a pen and a pad, a laptop, a post-it, or whatever I can get my grubby little hands on.

But now, emboldened with the confidence and knowledge that these words spring-clean my head and my heart, and better equip me for interacting with the world, I will be doing this for as long as I live, and with each word scribbled down, I know this for sure – being creative for creativity's sake fills the hole in my soul and is reward in and of itself.

Having processed all of this, I have to get going, as I am making up for lost time – I have to keeeeeeeep on truckin', driving it forward, as it will take me with it, it is teaching me all the time about the good, and the bad, things I have done in my life, who I am right now, and who I want to be in the future.

Rewriting defeats into victories takes a certain level of commitment, it means I have to trim the fat of the peripheral nonsense that can impose upon my life – it means, finally, I have little time for chit-chat, I can't leave it too late, here, you can have my DVD collection, I'll find out what the football score was later, sorry I can't stay longer, got to keep ironing out these creases, man. What can I say? These days, I guess I'm just an arsehole in a hurry.

SPRAY-CAN, CLIPPERS, & A PAIR OF OLD SLIPPERS

Hugh and Florence decided to down-size and move to a two bedroom terraced townhouse in the outskirts of the city – although their big old family house had grown quiet; what with the kids having all grown up and flown the nest, the sheer size of the grand old place meant that it had remained a relentless chore to upkeep none the less. The combination of four bedrooms lying empty and Hugh having had a major heart scare – moving to a smaller place seemed the logical way forward. With the townhouse being a new-build, the walls painted in nothing snazzier than white or magnolia, there would be less necessity to carry out repairs, something that previously Hugh had let stress him out more than it should have done. All in all, the new place would be less of a physical and mental task.

The first six months in the new place, overall, had gone well; the neighbours were pleasant enough and not too overbearing, which suited Hugh and Florence; as pleasant as they were, nattering over the garden fence had never really been their thing, as through the years they would tend to socialise on their own terms. Although, having previously had an abundance of room to move about, the new place required a certain economy of space and movement that took a bit of getting used to, but the most important thing was that Hugh's health had stabilised, and for the first time since he was a young lad, he had some hobbies. Spread out throughout the week he would attend a painting class, as well as regularly playing lawn bowls and golf. Florence was happy doing a bit of volunteer work in between catching up with her friends and family. Everything was in its place; life was pleasant and still.

Then it started – subsequent phases of the new housing estate were complete and almost overnight, children seemed to be everywhere. At first, Florence commented positively to Hugh, "that's nice, lots of young families starting out together. This would be a good place to raise kids, don't you think?" Hugh nodded in acknowledgement, quietly neither up nor down about the apparent influx of young-uns.

Hugh loved to watch David Attenborough's animal shows. All set; sat on his couch with his feet up, a warm cup of tea at the ready, the show starts. PUH-PUH, PUH-PUH. "What is that?" Hugh asked aloud. PUH-PUH, PUH-PUH, PUH-PUH. External to the side of Hugh and Florence's living room, was a pedestrian underpass. PUH-PUH, PUH-PUH. Hugh swiftly removed his feet from his footstool and firmly planted them on the ground, spilling some of his tea in the process. "Flo, someone is bouncing a ball off our wall. I'm heading out there right now to tell them to chuck it", Hugh declared to his wife, clearly agitated. His chest tightening, Hugh began to tug at his shirt collar, his heart racing. Florence sprang into the room. "Look at you, Hugh. You're getting yourself in a hell of state. It's just some kids. I'll go out and have a quick word with them. Please, just leave it to me." Florence said calmly, hoping to address the situation quickly and fully, as not to get out of hand and have Hugh getting too worked up about it. Florence, put her slippers on and went outside. Hugh paused the TV and went upstairs, as he thought he would be able to hear what was going on better from the window of the spare bedroom.

Florence went outside to find a pair of young twin boys, around thirteen or fourteen years old, and a girl who looked a couple of years older. Calmly, and with a warm smile on her face, Florence politely explained that her living room was on the other side of the wall that they were hitting their ball against, and then requested that they kindly stop doing it. Without skipping a beat, the twin boys in unison said "no", before the young girl, with her long blonde pigtails and a face that looked as though butter wouldn't melt in her mouth, informed Florence. "My Mum says that this is public property and we can play here if we like." Completely flabbergasted, Florence replied, "excuse me?" The girl, so completely sure of herself, replied, "and there is nothing you can do about it, we know our rights." Just then, Florence lost her temper and yelled, "bugger off the lot of you. Go on, scram!" The kids walked away, looking back as they did so, smiling and laughing. It was in that moment; the seeds had been sown; the war had begun. Florence and Hugh's house was now a target – to the new kids on the estate it would be the only thing that mattered, and if Hugh and Florence thought a bouncing ball was a nuisance, they hadn't seen anything yet. As it tends to be so often in life, Florence's initial decency was interpreted as weakness, and to be seized upon like prey by wild animals.

Night after night, more kids would gather, some as young as eight or nine years old, but most in their mid to late teens – the harassment getting worse and worse by the day. Each time Florence would beg Hugh not to get involved, and despite his fury, Hugh respected Florence's wishes – as he stood in silent contemplation by the spare bedroom window, as more and more the kids harassed and laughed at Florence. On one of the occasions, Hugh heard Florence plea, "please stop this, my husband is not a well man, he has acute angina." To which one of the boys snapped back, "what? Your husband has a cute vagina?" Followed by the unruly, moronic cackle of his friends and associates. Here was Hugh; a man of decency, who worked hard all his life; raising himself up from humble beginnings to have a successful career, to be a good father, and someone who lived a life of quiet dignity; always turning the other cheek in the face of obnoxious, aggressive, or unreasonable behaviour. And yet again, what was he to do to; just take it; just bow down; be forced to move home and cave-in to this lunacy: all because of a bunch of kids that should know better?

Then one night, after weeks of shouting and screaming, countless pieces of chewing gum being stuck on the wall and pavement outside, rubbish being put through their letter box, and dog shit being thrown in their back garden, Florence happened to be out visiting a friend. The hubbub outside was absolutely obscene; the worst yet. This could not go on, as after all; every man has his limits.

It was almost nightfall, and yet the unholy squadron of kids with nothing better to do, would not relent. During this reign of harassment, there had been nights where Hugh was unsure if he could take it, often leading him to double down on his medication. Although, not this time, as even though it was balmy summer's night, Hugh was perfectly cool and calm as he went upstairs and put on a long winter coat, a scarf around his face, and a black woolly hat upon his head. Easing his way downstairs, he pulled at the light chord of the cupboard under the stairs where he kept his tools. Eyeing up the hammer and screwdrivers, as tempting as they were, he felt a natural kick of restraint. Although, the red spray-can and Clover's old hair clippers looked absolute perfection. It broke Hugh's heart when they had to put Clover down, the loyal old dog that he was, and Hugh wondered why he ever kept Clover's hair clippers – "this must be why", Hugh concluded, certain that everything in life happens for a reason.

As Hugh slowly turned the front door key, just as he was about to walk out, he noticed Florence's slippers on the floor. "Oh, I'll have those too", he thought. Swiftly, Hugh made his way into the underpath, the kids didn't notice him at first, regardless, he presumed that he would be able to buy himself a few seconds and that they would not initially fear him as they had only ever encountered Florence. Just then, the kids were alerted to Hugh's presence when he started to shake the spray-can; like a metallic rattle snake, the kids froze where they stood. TICKA-TICKA-TICKA-TICKA – then TSHHHHHHH – Hugh sprayed red paint all over the face and hair of the two spotty little twin boys as he said, very matter of fact, "have that." They let out an almighty yell, then scarpered in floods of tears. Hugh turns his head, the little girl with the long pigtails was stood there, mouth agape, frozen in shock. NYYYYYYYYYYUUUH – hair clippers right down the middle of her head; inverted mohawk. "There you go", Hugh quipped. The kids all start running away in hysterics like Hugh was some kind of mythic-horror-film-creation. Although, one of the older boys stood firm, then came towards him. "Hey! What the fuck do you think that you're doing?" He asked, thinking that he was going to be the one to do something about this. Hugh reached into his pocket and – WHAAAACK – he smacked the young guy off his feet with one of Florence's slippers, adding, "oooft. Sore chops." The boy fell to the ground holding his face, before scrambling back up and then, like the others, running away as though his life depended on it.

Hugh stood alone in the underpass; an anti-hero done good – satisfied that justice had been served. But he couldn't hang around. Hugh began to walk away in the opposite direction from where the kids had gone, and as he made his way through the estate, discarding the coat, hat, spray-can, clippers, and slippers in various bins and bushes as he went, finally he arrived at his local pub in search of a victory beer. Sat in the pub, four pints in, he texted Florence, "Hi sweet heart. Went to pub. Don't wait up. XX"

The following day, the Police knocked on the door, asking if either Florence or Hugh had seen or heard anything the night before. Florence answered, as Hugh stood quietly at the top of the stairs. "I'm afraid I was out with friends, and my husband was down the pub for a rare night out", Florence explained. The officer added, "some kids who had been a bit of a nuisance; graffitiing and littering by all accounts, were assaulted last night, and ironically there is no CCTV footage as the victims were the ones who had broken the CCTV cameras weeks ago." The police officer then pressed further, "can I have a quick word with your husband?" Florence replied, "I'm afraid not officer, my husband doesn't keep very well, and he is sleeping just now. Perhaps some other time."

Reluctantly, the police officer left, handing over a business card with a contact phone number on it, should any piece of information spring to either Florence or Hugh's mind. As Florence locked the door, Hugh made his way down the stairs. Florence, keen to know, if Hugh had seen or heard anything, "oh, there you are. That was very strange, that was the police, they were asking if we saw anything going on last night. Apparently, those kids that have been bothering us were assaulted." Hugh replied, "Mhmm, that is strange. Strange indeed. Anyways, cup of tea? David Attenborough's on in a minute."

The next day, someone, whether it was the local council or whoever, jet washed all the chewing gum and graffiti from the underpass. Hugh got to watch his wildlife shows in peace – his tea was warm, his couch was comfy – and the kids never bothered Hugh and Florence ever again.

BOG-ROLL, JE T'AIME

This is a true story, although I wish that it wasn't. Waiting to take off from Glasgow Airport on a bright spring Monday morning, "the honeymoon starts here" I thought – "Paris awaits." I had been married for a couple of days now, and I was still absolutely buzzing. Our special day could not have gone better – all our nearest and dearest friends and family had gathered together to witness my stunning bride; elegance and grace personified, and me; a wee guy in a kilt, finally tie the knot.

The morning after the wedding, we opened our gifts and cards as we tried our best to chill-out in the midst of what was a hectic, but very exciting, time for us; going over every detail of the amazing day we had just shared together, and looking forward to our honeymoon; a few days in Paris; my wife's favourite city, followed by a few days in Munich; where neither of us had ever been before, before capping it all off with two days in one of our shared favourite cities on Earth, Berlin.

The flight took off, and with a day ahead of walking around the sheer massiveness of Paris, and with all the excitement of the past few days catching up on me, I tried to catch forty winks. I told my wife that I was going to catch some ZZZs, then I put my earphones in to listen to some music to ease me off to sleep, all seemed well with the world. However, I had only closed my eyes for a couple of minutes, when I felt this sudden, and very painful, ache in my stomach. Immediately, I began to feel faint, I had absolutely no idea what was going on. I muttered something to my wife about how I needed to go to the toilet. However, with military precision, the stereotypically, and undeniably, uber-camp male Flight Attendant had launched the drinks trolley down the aisle the second that the seatbelt lights went off, making my route to the toilet pretty much impossible, especially given the state of me. "Eugh! I can't handle this", I thought. Luckily though, as it was so early, very few people seemed to want a drink. That was until, the trolley got to just a row in front of me. "Anyone for drinks or snacks?" The Flight Attendant asked. "You need to let...me... You need let me." I whispered to him. My eyes were rolling ever so slightly. "Sorry sir, I can't hear you." He informed me, slightly perturbed at the low volume of my voice. I managed to generate one almighty, "you need to let me through, I think I'm going to faint."

The Flight Attendant juddered the trolley forward just enough to enable me to get out of my seat. I made my way as quickly as I could to the toilets at the front of the plane. All I kept thinking was, "you're going to faint. Just do it in the privacy of the John, no one needs to see this embarrassing farce that you have somehow got yourself into." Luckily, the toilet was vacant. I get in and, "what now? What is this? Am I having a heart attack?" The sweat lashing off me, I could feel the colour draining more and more from my face. I thought that it would probably be best if I sat down at least. Just then, as the result of the slightest bending motion, the demon that had consumed me had chosen the form in which it wished to manifest before being unleashed upon the world. Frantic, frenzied clawing madness, I drop my jeans, and oh sweet Lord – I begin to power-piss out of my arse. "Oh no, you absolute gimp!"

I think to myself. "We're on our honeymoon, this was never meant to happen, it was meant to be long walks and love making, red wine and live music, sight-seeing and hugs." But there I was, a ghoul of a man; having just succumb to a right nasty episode; my stomach aching, my t-shirt soaked through with sweat to the point where it looked like I had been thrown in a swimming pool – I cut a shambles of a figure.

I cleaned myself up. But instantly thought, "wait, there's more tummy-twitching, this madness might not be over, it may only have just begun." I put the toilet lid down and just sat there for a moment, hoping to pull myself together. The door knocks, and it's my wife. Having previously suffered from low blood-sugar crashes, my wife had an idea what might be wrong with me. I open the door to find my her, armed with the key essentials; a bottle of water and a Twix. All that I could do to reciprocate, was greet her with a wall of acidic-arse-death musk. But like an absolute legend, she didn't even acknowledge it. Although, over my wife's shoulder, I see a young woman who was queuing up to use the toilet, but having clearly seen the horrific state of me, she made the "oh, fuck that" face and opted to head to the toilet at the opposite end of the plane.

We arrive at Charles De Gaulle Airport. From the plane to the baggage collection, we had to walk down, what seemed like, an endless windowed corridor – the morning sun shining through and cooking me like I was under a magnifying glass. We eventually got to the end of the corridor when I noticed the Gents' toilets. I go in with the intention of doing a precautionary sit down, to see if anything happens and minimise the horror of the journey to the hotel. Sat there, gutted at the sudden change of events, I looked down and thought "my legs don't look real." I had never seen before, and I have not seen since, my skin colour look so unhealthy; a strange greenish, yellowy colour, and kind of waxy looking in texture, like I had swapped legs with Data from *Star Trek: The Next Generation*. Just sat there, waiting for the next round of soul-escaping arse trauma, there was nothing doing. I concluded "I just need to get on with this, and if another wave of this anal exorcism heads my way, I will just have to improvise."

My wife loves Paris, having fallen in love with it after she back-packed around Europe the summer that she finished high school. She loves everything about it; including the Metro. When we planned the honeymoon, we had both agreed that we would ease into the city and the experience of it all by getting the Metro to the hotel, but that was before this bout of intestinal anarchy. We collected our bags and made our way towards the exit, and there it was, a massive electronic map of the Metro system. I say this with zero hyperbole, but just the sight of it nearly made me shit myself, cry, and have a panic attack, all at the same time. "You get me on that thing, and I will fucking die", I thought to myself. Luckily, my wife, just from looking at me, knew that I really did not want to get on a series of underground trains in that physical and mental state. Thankfully, my wife said, "best to just get a taxi then", and if I wasn't leaking illness from every pore, I would have given her a big sloppy kiss.

We got into a taxi straight away. The lady driving was from Ghana or Ghanian origin, how I know this, is that she had about forty Ghana flag stickers dotted all over her car. We showed her a print-out with the address of our hotel on it, she nodded in acknowledgement, put the car into first gear, and began to drive so fast, and with such purpose, it was as though she was being pursued by the massive tripod alien spaceships from *The War of the Worlds*. Seeking some fresh air, I put the window down slightly, then a bit more, and then before I knew it, I had my entire head hanging out like I was a wee dog. The fresh cool air providing some much sought-after comfort, and the whole time I was thinking, "this will be handy if I think that I am going to be sick. And if it starts to come out of my bum, such is my fragile mental state, I may well just hang my arse out the window and subsequently secure my status as a disgrace of international proportions."

The driver continues to blaze through the city unfathomably fast; a couple of times we go into big tunnels that look identical to the one that Princess Diana died in, and I think to myself, "if I see a white Fiat tailing us, I'm out of here; tumble and roll style." It begins to rain a little; just a little spit. The driver, from her master controls, tries to put the windows up. I immediately retort with absolute index-finger conviction, "no way", I think to myself, we are the paying customer, and besides, all she had to do was look at the state of me; had she presumed that I was only in town to be humanely put down, I would have thought, "sure, I see where you are coming from."

We arrive at the hotel and it is a classy boutique joint. We are greeted at Reception by a very dapper looking gent who books us in quickly, and I notice as a nice touch, all the room keys have old doorknobs as key rings. The fellow behind the counter explains that we were never to leave the hotel without handing the key into Reception, as this was hotel policy.

Having made our way to our room, I immediately go for a bath, as they didn't have a shower, and I then I went for a kip in the hope that it would regenerate me. When I woke up, I got dressed and we decided to go for a short walk. When we got down to Reception, we handed in our room key. In English, but with a pleasant soft French accent, the Hotel man said, "have a beautiful evening. Enjoy Paris."

We made our way down the traditional narrow cobbled street that led to some nightlife; ahead the bars and restaurants beckoned us forward; to feel alive, to breathe in this most majestic of cities. But there is only one thing that I was feeling; that little bubble inside my stomach. I told myself, "you'll be fine. You will be fine. It's just going to be a little trouser-cough, your ring-piece has your back here, we're all good." And there, no more than twenty steps, and thirty seconds from our hotel; on the first night of our honeymoon – I sharted – as clean a follow-through as you can get. "About turn", I declared, very matter of fact. My wife, confused, "what is it?" "I have just shat myself. Quick, come on." We walk straight back into the hotel, the Receptionist clearly puzzled when we asked for our room key back, only having just given him it. It must have been, quite literally, the shortest night out ever.

Over the next few days that followed, with more baths and yet more sleep, we braved some of the sights, uncertain if my sphincter would have the will to behave itself on foreign soil. At the Louvre, the Mona Lisa smirked at my trouser misfortunes, while at Notre Dame Cathedral the ugly bastarding gargoyles looming from up on high were unsympathetic and out-right pass-remarkable; "and people say we look rough." Well, I don't know if that happened for sure; illness, a lack of food, and an ungodly amount of walking can do that to a man. Paris was frustrating, as we were looking forward to it so much, but it was hindered by a daft, yet all conquering, bug; a wee viral scumbag who robbed my wife and I of the full potential of the trip. As we got ready to leave, all set for Munich, not knowing what the future held, the one thing I knew for certain, and that has stuck with me until this very day – bog-roll, je t'aime.

"What do you mean, the offer's off the table?" Ronnie asked Mr Smith, in a tone a notch above even-tempered. Mr Smith, unmoved, "Ronald, at the eleventh hour of your application, it has come to our attention that you have a criminal record and that you spent some time in prison."

Confused, Ronnie sought to clarify matters. "Hold on a minute here. You told me that the background checks I completed were to weed out nonces, and I ain't no beast. So, what the fuck's the problem?" Mr Smith, remaining firm, "please, Ronald, there is no need for that kind of language here."

Mr Smith opens the palms of his hands to signify his intention to be open and transparent. "Yes, we do hope to protect the kids from, as you put it, 'beasts', but we also have to look at the type of role models that we allow to engage with them, especially impressionable young boys. A criminal record doesn't fit the profile of the coaches we have here at this academy — I know that this must be incredibly frustrating for you. However, it is company policy. There are no exceptions."

During their previous meeting, Ronnie had been really polished; confident, articulate, and affable. Now, Ronnie had to gather every ounce of inner strength he could muster to not just flip the table over and stick the nut in Mr Smith.

"Right, Mr Smith, here it is. When I was young, I was a bit of a boy; I loved drink and drugs, messing with birds I shouldn't have been, and wrecking folk every now and then. I loved the life and the life loved me. Then one time I bump into some mug who is just like me, only this time he catches me in a good mood. He started to try and wind me up, and no matter how much I told him to just walk away and sober up, he wouldn't let it go. He put his hands on me and I cracked him one — he went down, hit his head off the kerb, died instantly, and I went to jail for six years for manslaughter.

But see that daft, confused, angry boy that did that. He's gone, he's not the man you see before you; looking to be a positive influence, looking to help young boys and girls stay out of trouble by learning by my mistakes."

Mr Smith pauses for a moment to compose himself, now frustrated that Ronnie won't simply accept what he is saying to him. "Ronald, this organisation cannot overlook this matter. There is no room to manoeuvre – regardless of how much of a good word I put in for you, we cannot bend the rules."

Ronnie, enraged. "Show me him, show me him; the daft young boy that committed that crime. He's not here, it's just me. Look, I've got grey hair and crows' feet – that boy is gone, never to come back. What you're looking at is someone looking to integrate back into society, earn an honest living, and use my experiences to help others. For fuck sake, there's Holocaust survivors who have forgiven Nazi prison guards, and all I want is a job coaching weans how to play football."

"Ronald, I'm sorry. This is our final decision. This meeting is over. Good luck, and I hope that you find better fortune elsewhere." Mr Smith stands up and gestures to the door, "if you would please make your way out."

Ronnie burst out the building and onto the street. He reaches into his pocket and takes out his phone. He scrolls through his contacts for a minute before texting some of the boys from his old bit; to see what's happening. Afterall, there's nothing else for it – and besides, they're good boys, proper boys.

SHEILA

Robert loved his immediate family, but he was wary of family functions. He was twenty five, had been single for a couple of years now, and he was currently working in a temporary job – it 'ripped his knitting' to know that it was a certainty that his relatives would do their nosey, and if he were to reply truthfully, it would shed light on the aspects of life that he was dissatisfied with, when all he wanted was a couple of beers and some cheese and pickle on a stick.

Robert's aunts and uncles, generally, were personable, modern, and engaging. And then there was Aunty Sheila. Aunty Sheila was, for lack of a better description, a bit of an old fud. Despite having not been on a date, never mind been with a man, since The Godfather was first in movie theatres, she would always be the first to pry on Robert's love life; a relentless barrage of questions, that always concluded with her telling the same joke she had told him a thousand times before – "I've still not got a man – I should have emigrated to Australia, they love a Sheila over there. Get it? Sheila, they love a Sheila. Get it?" Being in her presence, Robert wanted to rip his own eyelids off and eat them as if they were crisps.

Robert, doing his best to let Sheila's noise breeze through him, took a second just to look at her. Robert thought to himself, "she's been rocking the same hair and make-up style since the 1970s; her bright eye-shadow made her look like a crazed exotic bird, her hair like a blonde See-you-Jimmy hat. Sheila – so over-baring and sinfully invasive, always laughing at her own jokes, a pathological need to be the life of the party – a diabolical human-like entity."

As is always the case on nights such as these, as Robert would make small talk with his cousins and the aunts and uncles that he liked, he knew with a certain degree of certainty that Sheila would demand a dance, most probably to ABBA, and Robert fucking hated ABBA. Not only that, Sheila used to get really fired up, a sensation brought on by the delusion that it was somehow funny, or "wacky", that a young guy would dance with his middle-aged aunty.

Enjoying a lovely cold beer, for a moment Robert quietly thought to himself that perhaps he had escaped Sheila's clutches.

And then "Waterloo" started. "Oh no", Robert said aloud, and just at that, Sheila grabbed his arm. "Oh, come on, Robert. Come on up for a dance." Dragging him forward, Robert noticed a pretty girl who he had never seen before, smiling at him, as they made their way to the dance floor. Sheila, and her cobra-like instincts spotted the electricity between Robert and the pretty girl, causing her to lean into the girl's face and declare, "I'm his favourite aunty, by the way. And I can dance him under the table." Robert was furious – furious that a more relaxed, tactful means of introducing himself to the girl had now been robbed from him.

Robert took a deep breath, "Sheila, you'll need to excuse me, I am desperate for the toilet." Sheila, unconvinced, "oh come on, Robert, I am sure you can hold in a pee for just one song." Robert started to jostle with Sheila, trying to break loose. "Come on now, Robert, don't be mean. I want my dance." Robert, a good bit more forceful, leaned into Sheila's ear, "I need to go! I'm bursting for a shite!" "Oh. I see", said Sheila, and with that, Robert made a bee-line for the toilet.

Robert didn't need the toilet, he was just fed up, fed up with Sheila's pish. His cousin, Alan, was a drug dealer, and although it was a family party, Robert knew that Alan would be carrying and no doubt lurking around the toilets. And there Alan was, "Alright, Robert. What's happening?" "Here's forty quid", Robert said as he planted the money firmly in Alan's hand. "I want something, anything. I don't need to know what it is – I just want to dance." Alan nodded, as if to say, "whatever man, it's on you", before he pulled out a small clear bag filled with pills of all shapes, colours, and sizes. As he placed a few of them in Robert's hand, Alan said, "that there is more than forty quid's worth, my man – call it 'family mate's rates', if you know what I mean?" Robert, having never taken a drug in his life, in one handful, threw the pills down his throat. "Wow, calm down ya fucking madman" cried Alan, alluding to some semblance of a conscience. "Never mind me" said Robert, "I've got a date with the dance floor."

Robert made his way to the bar and ordered a pint of ice-water. Drinking it in the one go, he wiped his mouth with his sleeve, slammed the empty pint glass on the bar and said aloud, "Sheila – where is she?"

Secure in his mind that his basic fitness levels would see him through the first few dances before the pills kicked in, Robert sought Sheila out like an enemy submarine. The drugs kicking in quicker than Robert anticipated, he spoke with a broad loud voice, like he was John Wayne. "Dance me under the table is it? That sounds like a challenge, Sheila." Sheila's eyes lit up, this would bring her some of the attention she so desperately craved. "Oh – you are on, Robert my boy."

A new song kicked in, Robert wasn't even sure what song it was, all he could feel was the beat; surging through him. He began to shake his arms and legs and once he started, he couldn't stop.

For the first few songs, Sheila kept shouting things like "I love it, Robert" and "whooo, you're wild." Then, a few songs more, trying to get in Robert's head, Sheila would ask, "getting tired yet?"

As other people would come and go from the dance floor, Robert and Sheila remained locked in their battle of wills. Eventually, the room picked up on what was happening and formed a circle around them.

Robert, now operating in numerous dimensions, knew only one thing for sure – just keep dancing.

So completely lost in the high and the sound, Robert had been dancing with his eyes closed for ages. When he eventually opened them again, he thought it must have been the drugs; that perhaps he was having a bad one, as when he looked at Sheila, she cut a monstrous sight; her mascara dripping off her chin, her lipstick smudged, her hair soaked in sweat and matted to her face; like someone had thrown a bucket of water over her.

Sheila's eyes widened, she looked straight at Robert, then fell into him. Trying to hold on, her hands on his triceps slipped down swiftly and she collapsed on the dancefloor.

The music stopped. "Quick, someone phone an ambulance, Sheila's having a heart attack" – the night was over, Robert had won.

Robert insisted on escorting Sheila in the ambulance, repeatedly being given into trouble by the paramedics for dancing and fidgeting about too much as they rushed to the hospital.

Sheila died on arrival.

At the funeral, Robert felt like the golden griever; somehow everyone forgetting that he thought that Sheila was a total pain in the arse. People would say things like "we know how close you were, and how you loved to dance together. If she could have chosen a way to go, I think that's what she would have wanted." Robert would simply reply "thanks", then think to himself "people don't half talk shite at funerals and do a ton of misremembering."

After the funeral, as everyone met to have some nibbles and a drink, the pretty girl from the party appeared. "It's Robert isn't it? I just wanted to say how sorry I am, you were so sweet to dance with your aunt all night long. It's just so sad." Robert leaned over and gave her a big hug, "thank you. I'm devastated, I'll never dance again." The girl squeezed Robert's hand, "come on, let's get you a drink."

As Robert and the pretty young girl held each other as they made their way to the bar, Robert thought "nice one. And I wonder if that mad old sort left me anything in her will."

I HAVE DIED 109 TIMES

"A coward dies a thousand times before his death, but the valiant taste of death but once."

— William Shakespeare, Julius Caesar

I have danced with cowardice on more than a few occasions; held her close, tasted her as she kissed me; seduced by her promise of sanctuary, and when our embrace drew to a close – I was discarded, left alone with nothing but regret and the sobering realisation that no matter which way I cut it, I hurt myself more than anyone.

It is important to remember those times when you saw the look in someone's eyes after a moment where you should have stood but instead you caved; you shirked, you passed the buck, you said nothing. Remember those moments, let them shame you into action, let them mould you into someone of substance – it is in this that you will realise your worth and gain respect from others, and yourself.

I am done with cowardice. Get it to absolute fuck.

EARTHERS

As the space shuttle, New Dawn, cleared its way through Earth's atmosphere, on board Agent De Vries turned to Agent Coyle, "I simply cannot wait to meet the settlers on Mars." Agent Coyle nodded in agreement. Agent De Vries continued, "those brave men and women – heroes one and all; pioneers, visionaries." Agent Coyle nodded in agreement once more, adding, "most certainly. Although, my heart breaks to know that we will never return to Earth." "Pah" replied Agent De Vries in complete disdain, adding, "not I. My heart has not softened since my application to the academy was approved. I will not miss it, nor a soul on it"

Agent Coyle, willing to give agent De Vries the benefit of the doubt, probed further. "Come on. Surely, there must be something or someone that you will miss. We have only been terraforming on Mars for a little over a decade and it is a million miles away from providing even a glimpse of what the Earth has to offer." Agent De Vries shook her head, "please, Agent Coyle, you cannot allow yourself to fall prey to nostalgia or be so short-sighted. Look at what we are doing, and why we are doing it – you and I have been given the honour of joining the largest concentration of elite human beings in existence; the smartest minds, the finest physical specimens, with a shared thirst for knowledge, and an unwavering commitment to science and progress."

Unimpressed by Agent De Vries's sentiment, Agent Coyle scowled, "I signed up to play my part in advancing our species; and to share what we will learn with those back home to enhance our mutual existence. I didn't sign up to be part of some interplanetary master race." Rolling her eyes, Agent De Vries declares, "my dear, you simply cannot afford to be this naïve, especially someone as gifted and intelligent as you", as she begins to walk away.

Furious, Agent Coyle raises her voice, "don't walk away from me. Please, enlighten me." Agent De Vries turns back to face Agent Coyle, slowly raising her hand to point to the window, to gaze at Earth once more as it gets further away in the distance. "Think about it – I am mean *really* think about it. It's over-populated, it's terminally ill – mankind has taken the finest creation fathomable and infected it like a parasite. We have an opportunity, us, the best humanity has to offer; it's premium stock, to cast concepts such as war, hunger, racism, you name it, and make them abstract, something to teach our children about on our new home as a history lesson, free from such needless waste, weakness, and destruction. When the Earthers mess it all up for good, and the planet goes up in smoke, we will be safe in the knowledge that it was us that not only saved our species but raised it up to an entirely different level."

As Agent De Vries turned and walked away once more, Agent Coyle's heart ached to know that Agent De Vries's lack of empathy was like a virus, a virus that would take hold in their new home, and that while they were leaving Earth behind, they could not abandon the folly of mankind.

DRAWERS

Declan came home from work at what had recently become his usual time; 17:30. He used to come home later, but these days he doesn't have to work such long hours.

Immediately, he was unnerved not to be greeted by the usual racket around the dinner table generated by his wife and three young daughters – instead, he was met with an eerie silence. Declan made his way into the kitchen to find his wife, Marie, sat alone with a shoe box in front of her on the kitchen table. Marie's face is solemn, her lips pinched. "Where are the kids?" Declan asked, knowing deep down that they have been extracted from the situation to enable whatever is about to unfold here to present itself. Marie replied, "they are staying at my Mum's tonight, I told her that we need to talk." "About what?" Declan asked, fearing the worst.

Marie leaned forward and opened the shoe box on the kitchen table. "I found these, Declan; designer shoes. Your third pair in as many months." Indignant, Declan replied, "aye, and what?" Marie continued, "but it's not just the shoes, is it? The new car, the clothes, the gifts for me and the kids. Six months ago, we were struggling to pay the bills on your electrician's salary, and then came all this. I feel so stupid, I can't believe it's taken me this long to figure it out. You're punting coke, aren't you? And don't fucking lie to me." Stood there, expected to say something, anything, in reply to Marie's accusations, Declan paused for a moment, and for a second he considered conjuring up some tall tale, but then decided to come clean. Declan walked over to the kitchen table and took a seat directly across from Marie.

Keen to put the drug pusher theory to bed, Declan lays the foundations of his retort. "Marie, sweetheart, I know what it looks like. But trust me, I am 100% not involved in any drugs or anything like that. However, clearly, I am making money on the side, and yes, I am selling something, but it's not drugs." Impatiently, Marie demanded more information from Declan. "Well, what is it then?" Declan bowed his head for a moment, before lifting his head once more and looking Marie right in the eye. "Sweetheart, I'm selling my drawers." Confused, Marie sought further clarification. "Drawers?

33

What, like furniture?" Declan, somewhat frustrated that Marie did not understand immediately what he meant. "No, not furniture – I am selling my worn pants to perverts on the internet. "Oh, my God, my husband's gay!" Marie yelled aloud. Declan, letting out a nervous giggle, "I'm not gay."

"Tell me, Declan. Tell me everything!" Marie demanded. "Alright, alright. About six months ago, as you know, no matter how much overtime I did or how many homers I did, it never seemed to be enough, we were always chasing our tails – we were eeking by, week-to week and sometimes day-to-day.

I did something that's really unlike me; frustrated, tired, and fed up, I had a wee moan online. I posted something about having finished an eighty hour week, being knackered, soaked through with sweat, skint, feeling like I had nothing to show for it. And five minutes later, I got this private message saying, 'nice profile pic, bro.' I replied, 'sorry?' He then came back to me and said, 'let's cut to the chase – you said you were soaked through with sweat after a hard week at work. How much for your pants?' I thought that this guy had to be winding me up, so I told him, 'here's my sort code and account number, put a hundred quid in my bank and we'll talk. And he did.

The next day I put my stinkin' dirty pants in a sealed sandwich bag and sent it to him via a courier. From there, he told me that he was part of an online community. In a way, he became a bit of a mentor to me; he recommended that I get my own website, upload some pics to it, and that he would be sure to promote me to his cash-rich friends within the community. Not to brag, but I've always kept myself in good nick and as you know – I'm quite well endowed – I mean, you always seemed to like my big baws."

Marie, her mouth agape, completely in shock. "Let me get this right – you're selling your dirty boxer shorts to dirty old men? You're disgusting." Declan, desperately hoping for some sense of reason. "Hold on, I didn't go looking for this. It's an opportunity that fell on my lap."

Marie went into her pocket and pulled out her phone, hastily thumbing her security code and opening a web browser. "What's your website?" Declan, somewhat embarrassed, "it's www.hotdrawers.club"

Marie scanned the website frantically, "it says here, you offer a premium service. What's that?" Declan replied, "some of my clients, who around eighteen percent happen to be female by the way, sometimes put in an order for a bit of extra 'character.'" "Character?" Marie enquired, completely bemused. Nervously smiling, Declan replied, "you know – some of them want...a bit of pee stain, or a bit of love-juice-snail-trail, and then there's the odd wild one that likes a right good old fashioned... skid-mark."

"Get out!" Screamed Marie. "Get out of this house, right now!"

"Alright, alright. I'll leave, but before I go, I want you to look at this." Declan reached into his pocket, took out his phone, entered some details, and then held the screen up to Marie's face. Marie's eyes widened once more, "does that say what I think it does?" Declan nodded, "yup, that there is my savings account – 16k sitting there, and that's despite all the gifts I've been buying and the new car."

Declan stood up and made his way to the front door, "Marie, I'll call you in the morning." Before turning the ignition of his car to leave, Declan booked himself into a 5 star hotel, once there he stayed up most of the night watching multiple episodes of Frasier and eating room service.

In the morning, Declan called Marie. "What's all that noise? I thought you would be at home." Sounding more than a tad sheepish, Marie replied "I'm in that new discount sport shop – buying you a couple of dozen pairs of boxer shorts."

Six months later, Declan, Marie, and the kids went an all-inclusive, no expense spared, holiday to Disneyland. Six months after that, they put the deposit down on their dream home; in the nice part of the town where Marie grew up, where she never dreamed that she would ever be able to afford.

Declan has no idea how long he can make this gig last, but together, he and Marie are going to give it their best shot. Declan bought a top-of-the-line camera and has hired a personal trainer to help him get in even better shape, while Marie has enrolled for a night class in Online Marketing.

Perhaps, sometimes we are faced with certain realities that initially horrify or freak us out, and then when we see the full picture – we realise that we are all malleable when the juice far exceeds the squeeze – and luckily for Declan, he knows that he has cash-rich fanbase that love it when he squeezes they juices.

A MAN OF HIS TIME

"Mad Jim" MacGregor was a local legend. All the kids loved to sit around and listen to his stories. You see, to these boys and girls, football was everything, and Mad Jim was like a God to them; the local lad who had travelled thousands of miles to rub shoulders with some of the best players who had ever lived.

Mad Jim's two sons would burst with pride each time he would regale the local pubs and parks with tales of his adventures to an ever engaged, enthusiastic, and star-struck audience.

An economy of words was not Mad Jim's strongpoint; he loved to talk about his life in great detail, and for as long as he'd talk, you'd be sure that there were plenty of folk more than willing to listen. Mad Jim would always begin his story by saying how heartbroken he was when, despite it being the most celebrated era in football north and south of the border; with England having won the World Cup the year before, and Celtic having just become the first team from the UK to win the European Cup, in 1967 Mad Jim was released by Motherwell F.C.

Mad Jim thought his dreams were in tatters – there he was; eighteen years old and unsure whether or not he had a future in the game or if it was now time to look for work in the shipyards.

But luckily for Mad Jim, after a couple of trials, he secured a season's terms at St. Mirren F.C, before eventually moving down south and becoming a bit of a cult hero at Port Vale F.C.

Then in 1975, at the age of twenty six years old, Mad Jim MacGregor was made an offer he couldn't refuse. Having hoped to be signed by one of the top English First Division clubs, back when that was the top league before the Premier League's inception, Mad Jim was called into his Manager's office to be told that Port Vale had received an offer from an American club called Dallas Tornado – a four year contract, on rock star money, plus a nice house and a Cadillac.

Mad Jim would explain how his eyes nearly popped out his head upon hearing the news. "Dallas? Texas? Do Americans even play football", he asked his gaffer. His boss replied, "they do indeed, laddie. It's called the North American Soccer League and these bloody Yanks are throwing fortunes into it. Signing up some top talent too, trying to convert the masses away from Baseball and the likes." Slowly nodding his head, Mad Jim said "Dallas, eh. I always considered myself a bit of a cowboy." And with that, Mad Jim MacGregor from the Gorbals in Glasgow, boarded a first-class British Airway Flight from London to Dallas.

From 1975 until 1979, Mad Jim lived the American Dream; basking in the sunshine, cruising around in his car that was as wide as a Scottish street, and getting to "meet" the scores of beautiful women that Dallas had to offer.

When people would ask him about some of the guys he played against, Mad Jim would gush, "some of the best ever, and I mean, *the* best ever." And when people would ask in disbelief, "Pelé?", Mad Jim would reassuringly nod, and say "aye. Yeah, I played against him, a couple of times – he actually gave me his shirt once, but we lost it in the house move of 82' when we moved from Bothwell to Partick. Oh, how I wish I had been able to hold on to that one. Would be worth a fortune now, I imagine."

Mad Jim would explain that although he moved to Dallas in 1975, the same year as Pelé, the next year they were joined by the Northern Irish maestro, and Manchester United legend, George Best. But it didn't end there; in 1977, West German legend, Franz Beckenbauer, "the Kaiser", signed on, as did one of Pelé's Brazilian team mates, the legendary Carlos Alberto, and to top it off, in Mad Jim's final year in the states, "The Dutch Master", Johan Cruyff arrived.

The crown of being local hero can be a heavy burden to some, but not to Mad Jim. He loved it; revelling in every moment, he never tired of talking about the games, the players, and the lifestyle.

However, matters soon got somewhat muddied for Mad Jim in the 1990s, when having been completely enchanted by tales of Mad Jim's footballing adventures, one of his sons' pals, Terry Cohan, asked if he could do a school project about him. Mad Jim was honoured to help a young local boy out.

Terry was like a dog with a bone, before going over to Mad Jim's house to interview the man himself, Terry sought to do a bit of online research, and what he found was – nothing. All the details of

Mad Jim's time playing football in Scotland and England was there, but that is where the trail went cold. Terry was able to find the Dallas Tornado team photographs for the seasons of 1975 -1979, and despite Mad Jim's imposing and unmistakable figure, Terry couldn't identify him in any of the pictures. The same element of mystery applied when Terry obtained the team roster for each season Mad Jim claimed to be there; no note of a Jim or James MacGregor to be seen anywhere.

Terry felt terrible; here he was, just looking to get a good grade on his school project, only to find himself with the knowledge that for all these years, the odds were, that the legend, Mad Jim MacGregor was a fraud; a fantasist – that all his stories of glory and getting to play against some of the best players in the world were merely a figment of his imagination. Terry knew that if Mad Jim had no reasonable explanation for his absence from the records, and if he exposed his fraud, it would ruin Mad Jim and his status within the local community. Terry desperately wanted the stories to be true, regardless of how big a scoop it would be to prove otherwise.

Armed with his pen and brand new blank A4 pad of lined paper, Terry went around to Mad Jim's house on a Sunday afternoon. Nervous, Terry had concluded that he would let Mad Jim have his say before deciding which way the story should unfold.

Sat in Mad Jim's living room, they shared small talk for a bit; the conversation was easy and free flowing, as every five minutes Mrs MacGregor would pop in to replenish the plate of biscuits and the cups of tea.

Eventually, Terry began his questions; starting with Mad Jim's time playing in the UK. As enthusiastic as Mad Jim was, he did not tell Terry anything that he didn't already know through his research.

Eventually, the conversation moved on to Mad Jim's time in America. "So, Jim, you played against some of the best players in the world, at that time. How do you reckon that they would compare to the superstars of today?" Mad Jim, smiling, "it would be hard to say really – I guess all you can ever be is a man of your time."

Terry knew that this was it; this was his chance to lay the evidence bare and really put Mad Jim on the spot and hear what he had to say for himself. But looking up at Mad Jim's face; so engaging and full of warmth. "Jim, I.. eh. I wanted to ask you another thing about your time in the states. I… I wanted to know…" Mad Jim laughed, "go on son, spit it out." Completely torn, Terry just sat there, frozen. Eventually, composing himself enough to say, "what I really need to know is… what's it like to drive on the other side of the road?" Mad Jim let out a hearty laugh. "Oh, a piece of piss son, you get used to it in no time."

Terry thanked Mad Jim and his wife for their time and their hospitality and then made his way home. A week later, Terry handed in his school report and got a B+.

No matter what, Terry thought "that mad auld rascal has probably been spinning a yarn all these years. And one day someone probably will expose him – but not me. Not now, not ever"

In the years that passed, every now and then, people would ask Terry, "is that right that you know Mad Jim MacGregor?" and with a wry smile, Terry would answer "I certainly do – great player he was; played against some of the best in the world." And when, inevitably, Terry was asked how Mad Jim would compare to players playing today, Terry would remember the big man's words – "it's hard to say – you can only ever be a man of your time."

WHERE DID YOU GO?

You've been dead for two days now. The pleasant Gent that greeted me upon my arrival here brought me no comfort; when he told me not to be afraid; that you were just how I would remember you; that it was as though you were only sleeping.

But this, this shape of a man that lies before me – this isn't you. This is a million miles away from you – and I am still trying to catch the air that was sucked from my lungs when I got the call about your passing. I cannot navigate this uncanny valley – in all our years together, I saw you sleep many times, but this; this is no blissful slumber, this is merely an empty vessel – this is not you.

Life has knocked God out of me – in the weight of your absence; this crater in my heart feels too deep, too wide, too much to bear – and I don't know if I have the tools to claw myself out.

Look at this place; so cold and clinical – the complete antithesis of you. You'd hate it here, I'm sure you'd crack wise, make your excuses, then make a swift exit. But what does it matter? You're not here anyway.

You were always warm blooded; a sweaty bloody mess – I can't bring myself to touch what lays here, not even for a second. Your fire, your song, your laugh, your talents, your kindness, your dreams, your smelly feet, your snoring, and your bad jokes – where are they now? If there is some cosmic pool, made up of all the souls that ever lived, it is enriched to have you there.

In a few days, we'll all gather round to mark your passing, and from there we are expected to go on. The world will keep on turning, it will not pause, not even for a second, to give me a single moment to plead your case – regardless of how much I wish it would.

Taken too young, the blockades across the infinite roads of possibility that your life could have taken you are cemented firmly in place. This pain inside of me is for us both – oh how I would love to meet and embrace you further down the line.

It has only been a couple of days and I already miss you more than you could ever know, my brother, my friend – until we meet again, I will always be searching for you.

DANIEL DAY LEWIS

Shane asked his Mother, Jean, "where's Dad?" Jean rolled her eyes, "that bloody mad man has been up since the crack of dawn, making a right bleedin' racket. God knows what he is up to." Clearly surprised, Shane commented, "Up early? I don't remember Dad ever getting up early in my entire life."

Shane's father, Ken, walks from the kitchen into the living room to find Shane and his wife there, "oh, hello son", before asking Jean, "sweetheart, do we have any heavy-duty bin bags?" Before Jane is able to reply, Shane looks his Dad up and down, totally confused by what stands before him. "Dad, what are you wearing? Where is your beard? What's with the track suit and gloves. Are you feeling alright?" Ken replies, "Daniel Day Lewis". Shane snorts with laughter, "the actor? what about him?"

"Well, last night your Mum had gone to bed and I stayed up to watch the snooker that I had recorded. Once that was finished, I decided to do a spot of channel surfing and it was there that I stumbled across a biography on one of the movie channels about Daniel Day Lewis. As I sat there, I was just amazed. I mean, this guy, he's just fantastic; he doesn't just play a character – he becomes the character.

I sat there as one after another, Directors and actors marvelled at his commitment, his craft, his sheer will and determination to manifest into an entirely different person, Then I looked down at myself – I am man enough to admit it, I began to weep uncontrollably; my big thick messy curly beard, filled with traces of last night's dinner, my big fat belly, my dirty nicotine stained finger nails. Then I thought about how I have been on the brew for nearly forty years – FORTY YEARS. You know that I have never been keen to talk about it, but when Thatcher robbed this town of its industry, it robbed us of everything. This place never recovered, and neither did I – seeing that I was just a number, just a single drop of water in a wave of collateral damage imposed upon the hard-working people of this country, the depression consumed me. But not now – "Daniel Day Lewis" – that is the battle cry.

I've shaved my face, I've cut the grass, I'm nipping out later for a big walk and to get a haircut and some nicotine patches. I'm leaving this character that I have been typecast as and I am becoming someone else, something else, and that's all there is about it."

"I don't know if you're taking this piss or not, but I'm right behind you, Dad. Come here." And with that, Shane gave his father a big hug. "Right lad, settle down. I don't have time for this mooshy claptrap – I'm a busy man now. See you later for dinner; steamed veg and chicken – no more shitey junk food."

Ken made his way outside, and without looking back, "Shane, remember! Daniel Day Lewis! Daniel Day Lewis!" And as Ken made his way down the street, Shane stood by the door, and as his Dad faded into the distance, he could still hear him repeating "Daniel Day Lewis! Daniel Day Lewis" getting quieter and quieter the farther away he got.

As Shane walked back into the house, he caught his reflection in the oven, and he thought to himself, "might as well give it a go…"

BREW

After university, it was time to look for a full-time job. There seemed to be a common misconception among my fellow graduates and I, that the part-time jobs that helped us out during our studies were suddenly beneath us, the moment we were qualified. To hold our degrees in our hands, it felt like a key to a world filled with stacks of disposable cash and opportunities.

But, as I have found at most stages in life, things didn't go as I had expected – some things work out better, some things pan out worse, but more often than not, things just work out differently from what I had envisaged.

Here I was, qualified and still stacking shelves in a supermarket at night, I thought to myself, "hang on a minute here – this isn't right." This sense of entitlement; it would soon be knocked out of me.

I bumped into a girl I grew up with, she had been living away for a year or two. As we made small talk, catching up with each other, she mentioned that she worked for the Department for Work and Pensions, and that they were recruiting. When she asked me if I would be interested in applying, I said yes, certain that if I got the job, it would be good experience and my first step into working life, and from there I could hunt down the role that would reflect my expectations.

I filled out an application and submitted it. Probably easier than it ever should have been, I was offered a three months full-time contract that soon became a permanent role.

Once I realised that people weren't going to throw shit-hot jobs my way, there had been a spell where I worried that I might end up on the brew, and here I was, working for the brew.

My job title was First Contact Officer. It was a large contact centre, the purpose of which was to support the new process of making a claim; via telephone interview, as the Government deemed the nation's unemployed, sick, and unfortunate, too inefficient in their form-filling skills. And despite it being an effort to minimise the use of paper, there were still piles of it, absolutely everywhere.

After a couple of weeks' worth of training, I was ready to go. I thought, "how hard could it be?" And besides, my Mum worked in social work for years, one of my brothers worked in housing, my other brother supported adults with special needs – I was just following a tradition of supporting vulnerable people in the community. Well, not really, I fell into this job, there was no grandiose plan to be a helper of others – this was not about any sense of social conscience or justice, this was about logging in, grinding out, and emailing my CV on my lunch break.

My first call, you could not have made it up. I was hoping for a couple of really simple calls to ease me in; young person, no kids, no job history, no savings, still lives with their parents – they were a breeze, the kind of call you want when your phone rings four minutes before your shift ends

But no, the first call to come through to me was a woman in her late thirties, she tells me that she lives in a big fancy house in a nice part of town, however, she has four kids and her husband has just come home and told her that their marriage is over and that he is leaving, and she doesn't have a bean to her name. As much as I think to myself, "this poor woman", I am completely exposed, in that all the training on how to support lone parents has completely disappeared from my mind. This poor woman; in the depths of despair, the universe has aligned so that of all the people she could have been put through to, she's been put through to me; a goon trying to survive his first day on the job, struggling to work the phone system – a total cabbage.

I apologise and explain that, unfortunately, it is my first day on the job. I put her on hold and seek the advice of my supervisor, such is the severity of the call, my supervisor redirects the call to his phone to get me off the hook and ensure that the woman is given the best, and most reliable, advice.

I'd love to say that calls like that were rare, but the sad thing is, they're not. Ten hours a day, five days a week spent submerged in a pool of people toiling with major financial worries, or too unfit to work, or struggling with substance abuse, or unable to work as they were somebody's carer, or unable to function due to a bereavement

– I spoke to them all, and it was clear from the off – I didn't have the stomach for it.

It was a real eye opener, supporting people whose situation was a bit alien to me. But it wasn't all misery, guts and chaos, sometimes you would speak to people whose lives were so interesting to me; one time, I took a call from a girl who was between jobs, she worked as a costume designer in film and TV, and she had just finished working on one of the Star Wars prequels – this completely blew my mind; someone got paid to work on a Star Wars film – I would easily donate my scrotes and spend my life as naked furniture in some pervert's dungeon just to walk on to the set of a Star Wars film.

There were calls that left me baffled; a guy quit his job because his boss said that he was no longer allowed to smoke in the work's van – that's all. In a way I admired his freedom; he had always smoked in his van when at work, now he wasn't allowed to, so he bowed out, just like that. Just the thought of such boldness brings me out in a cold sweat.

Then there were calls that were just outrageous. I spoke to a guy who was just out of jail, when he told me that he was unfit to work, it was part of my job to ask him the specifics of his ill-health. "I have hepatitis B, hepatitis C, and depression after I was shot in the groin by a policeman on a helicopter." I had to set my phone to mute – I laughed my arse off. I couldn't believe what I was hearing, the part about the helicopter, was it real? For the guy claiming to have been shot in the goolies, I hope not. But it was the sheer randomness of what I was being told that had me buckled.

But all in all, I worked for the Department for Work and Pensions for nearly three years. Undeniably, I dealt with a few scroungers; disenfranchised people who felt as though the tax payer owes them a living – but not many, and nowhere near what the more cynical and judgemental people in society would have you believe. But now, well over ten years on, I am not comfortable with the word "scrounger." Some people are born into a second, third, fourth generation of communities and families completely engrained in the welfare state, and who have never been granted the opportunity to gain the perspective to see that a better quality of life is available to them.

47

By the time I left the Department for Work and Pensions, I was cooked – it was making me ill – I could not switch off after the long days being inundated with tails of misfortune, woe, and tragedy. Unlike my Mum or my brothers, I wasn't even speaking to people face-to-face – I guess I just don't have that special something; that substance that enables you to aid the most vulnerable in society and still be able to come home and function without battle-damage when you clock out and go home to sit on the couch.

To the nurses, the carers, the doctors, the coppers, the volunteers, and anyone else who provides a service that supports the community, fair play to you – you are heroes, you tread where I don't have the guts to hang.

THE MALE FEMINIST

TO THE GIRLS

...I am here for you my sisters.

...I stand with you in your struggle.

...allow ME, and male feminists like me, to apologise on behalf of all men for everything that we have done.

...you can talk to me

...I repeat, I am here for you.

TO MYSELF

...those beastly brutish boys and their bulging biceps.

...they may have gotten their way before, but not anymore.

...I'll manoeuvre my way in, and we'll see who is laughing then.

TO THE GIRLS

...I am not a sexual threat to you.

...we can be besties, and I can show you that men and women can be just friends.

...let us embrace and heal each other.

TO MYSELF

...yes, I've wormed myself in, you won't know what's hit you.

...I have needs too.

...I'll do whatever, and say whatever, to get what I want.

...because I am a man, and I will say any old shit to get what I want.

TODAY'S AGENDA

The car will be here in a minute. Just this tie to put on and I will be ready to go, ready for the day ahead. Oh yes, that looks splendid; I love the sight of my blue tie, perfectly complimented by my crisp white shirt. Wife is remarkable; I simply do not know how she keeps my shirts and suits looking so sharp, not to mention my shoes; as shiny as mirrors one and all. No matter when or where I am sought for a media spot, I know that I am always more than capably attired.

I am feeling refreshed, the debate in the Commons yesterday went as well as I or the party could have hoped, and I was home early enough to enjoy a rare full night's sleep.

I make my way downstairs, and stood by the door is Wife and child, primed and ready to bid me a fond farewell. Wife enquires as to today's agenda, and when I inform her that I am to make an appearance at the opening of a new food bank for some photo opportunities and to mingle with the community before heading back to the office, it reminds her, "well, make sure that you have something in your tummy if you are going to the gym later." Dearest Wife, ever so thoughtful.

The car arrives and I kiss Wife on the cheek and pinch child's nose – just to look at him, I am bursting with pride to know that he will grow up in a Great Britain worthy of its esteem – that is what I work towards every day, for him, and those like him.

Peter greets me with an enthusiastic "good morning, sir" as he opens the rear passenger door of the car. As I fasten my seatbelt, the car sets off. Peter seems in good spirits, however, his voice shifts to a more serious tone when he talks about what our upcoming appointment. "Sir, I must warn you. We will probably take a bit of heat today." "How so, Peter?" I enquire. "These food banks, sir, they are becoming more and more prevalent and the opposition are claiming, most vociferously, that they are the direct result of many of our policies." Tosh! Utter nonsense. I simply cannot abide the lazy thinking of those bleeding hearted lefties. "Peter, when will these people understand that austerity is the only way that this country will keep its house in order, and that we simply cannot spend that which we do not have. So, a few families here or there

51

have some cash flow problems — it is testament to those hard-working, up-standing, people of Great Britain who are willing to volunteer to make sure that those unfortunate families, who are in a bit of a jam for a brief spell, have a means of assistance. Frankly, I do not understand all the hullabaloo — I guess those in opposition will dig their claws into anything — their point-scoring is so tiresome, so transparent."

That extra rest last night has worked wonders. Before today, the past few photo-ops I thought that I was perhaps looking a tad run-down, but today I was looking more like my old self, and having gotten that meet and greet with the public out of the way, despite a few quibbles, mumps, and moans — I am feeling energised and ready for what the afternoon brings.

Damn it, I have forgotten my earphones for the gym later. Mmhm, that is rather annoying. "Peter, could you be a star and pick up some earphones for me before I set off for my work-out? Just put it on my account." "Certainly, sir", Peter replies without hesitation. "Oh, and Peter, what does tomorrow's schedule have in store?" Peter reaches for his smartphone and after a few taps, he accesses the calendar function. "You have two hours set asides for constituent correspondences, and then at 12:30 you have a lunch and drinks with Clarence." Lunch with Clarence, how marvellous.

CONFIDENCE

I am apprehensive of no other state of mind like I am about confidence. The process tends to go:

have little to no confidence

build a bit of confidence

become capable

gain more confidence

get cocky

eat shit and die

learn humility

…and repeat.

THE FORBIDDEN FIRST-AIDER AFFAIR

I left Glasgow Central Station and made my way across the road to 54 Hope Street. I was feeling good; it was a break from the norm to be away from the office for the day, even if it was only to go on a first aid refresher course. I was sure that the training would be straight-forward; seeing as this would be the third time in six years that I had renewed my first aid certificate.

I made my way up to the third floor and got settled. After everyone on the course introduced themselves, we start to talk about our first aid experiences and any relevant anecdotes. The morning seemed to draw out a bit; mainly as it was more theoretical, and less engaging than the practical side of things.

As it neared noon, one of the two instructors announced to the class, "we'll be breaking for lunch in two minutes. When we come back, we'll introduce you to...", and as she removed a cloth from the object sat on the table, she declared, "...our manikin. Who we like to call, Big Frank."

At lunch, I phoned my wife, Linda, and asked how the girls were getting on. When Linda started to go into detail about the girls' day, she could tell I was distracted – and she was right, my mind was elsewhere; my mind was transfixed with the manikin I just met with the insatiable, hypnotising, "come fuck me eyes".

I couldn't wait to get back to the training centre after lunch. The instructors notified us that after a brief chat, the class would take turns at working on Big Frank. Such was my eagerness to be the first in the que, my head was a bit frazzled, leaving me not suitably prepared to navigate the natural flow of everyone in the class crissing and crossing, and to my despair, I found myself at the back of the que.

The green-eyed monster had me in it its grips; as one after another, people leaned forward and pumped Big Frank's broad chest, and then to make matters worse; they put their lips to his. How fucking dare they? The jealousy was tearing out of me. But it brought me some comfort to know that between exercises, Big Frank could not stop looking at me; his eyes, they followed me around the room like a sexy masculine limbless Mona Lisa.

After what felt like an age, it was my turn to be with Big Frank – he looked at me, as if to say "finally, you're here." I worked his chest, and with each compression, the more my hands began to tremble – counting down to the moment when I knew that, finally, my lips would touch his. And then we kissed – it felt so wrong, and yet so right. But what was I thinking, I'm a married man – but this, I had never known anything like it; the passion, the ecstasy stirring up inside of me – I was willing to give it all up, for Big Frank.

As the course ended, we filled out the feedback forms and made small talk. I took my time, making sure the rest of the class left before me, until it was only the instructors, Big Frank, and I left. I pretended that I needed to quickly nip to the Gents' before I left, the course instructors duly obliged as they retreated to a back room. Having noticed a CCTV camera facing outwards from the front door of the training centre, I ran from behind it, jumped up, and yanked the cable out. I saw my opportunity, and as to make sure that Big Frank was not cold, I wrapped him in the very same sheet that he had been concealed in before he was revealed to me earlier.

I ran a few blocks until I came to a hotel – Big Frank and I had some unfinished business. I paid for one of their most expensive rooms; jacuzzi, the lot. Once we got in the room, Big Frank and I couldn't take our hands off each other – it was all so new and dangerous; I had never been with a man before, especially one with only a torso and head, and who never speaks.

Throughout the night, I held Big Frank in my arms – we rolled around entwined; on the bed, the floor, in the jacuzzi, and in the shower too. At one stage, Big Frank's chest compression clicker was clicking so much I wondered if he could handle it. I told him, "I know that you have kissed countless numbers of people, but I don't care. It only matters that you're here with me now."

Every now and then I would notice my phone lighting up; my wife, Linda looking to see where I was and if I was okay, but I ignored her; she simply wouldn't understand.

In between the physical stuff, I would talk and talk and talk, and Big Frank was more than happy to listen. We were in the middle of a really deep and meaningful conversation when I noticed Linda calling once more – so I put my phone on the floor and battered it with my shoe, declaring "farewell my love, it was good while it lasted." And while the kids would be upset at my abandoning them, in the years to come when they were older, I am sure that they will understand.

As the sun began to peek through the curtains at dawn, the light illuminated Big Frank as he lay in my arms. It was then that I told him, "I've never felt this way about anyone." And he just looked at me knowingly, as he does, and I knew that he felt the same.

We check out of the hotel and took an early morning stroll through the city. It is surreal to see the Glasgow so quiet and calm, the sunshine making us drunk with the optimism of the amazing possibilities of what the day could bring.

We knew that we needed to get away – that we were going to start a new amazing life, together. Arriving at Buchanan Bus Station, I noticed a bus going to London. London; we could blend in there, I thought, start afresh. I buy both Big Frank and I a ticket and I make my way to the back of the bus. I nipped back down to the front of the bus to ask the driver how long it would be before we set off on our journey. The bus driver told me "it should be five minutes, however, I need to nip to the Gents' so don't hold it against me if we are a minute or two late." I walked back up to Frank and told him, "it's you and I now. But, I feel I owe Linda some kind of explanation. There is a pay phone right there, I am just going to give her a quick call, and then I will be back in time for us to set off and start our new life together." Big Frank looked at me, the sheer empathy bleeding from his eyes.

I put a few coins into the pay phone and called Linda. As I waited for her to pick up I remembered how, for the past few years, I have occasionally wondered who still uses pay phones, and then I realised, it's people like me; people who have freed themselves from the tyranny of their mobile phone, free to pursue their dreams without Big Brother knowing their every movement.

When Linda picked up, she sounded absolutely dreadful; "where are you? Are you okay? I was just about to phone the police – the girls and I are worried sick." I told Linda that I was sorry, that I had met someone and it was "the lightening bolt"; the one true connection, that I was sorry for hurting her, and that I hoped that both she and the girls would forgive me in time, as after all; the heart wants what the heart wants.

As Linda screamed down the phone at me, the phone beeped to tell me that I was running out of credit, and I had no more change in my pocket. "Linda, I have to go. Tell the girls that I love them and that I am sorry, but I am off to start a new life."

I put the phone down and bowed my head – sometimes, in the pursuit of happiness we have to let someone go. I turned around to make my way back to the bus, and instantly, my heart sank; there was the bus to London, the doors shutting. "Wait, Wait!" I cried. But the bus was unobstructed, it started moving, then picked up pace. "Wait! Please wait!" I shouted louder, then again louder still. "Don't go!"

With my head down, I chased the bus as fast as I could, but to my dismay there was a break in the traffic and the bus accelerated away. I looked up, dejected, "Frank! Big Frank" I yelled.

I was devasted. Just then, to make matters worse, some kids got a hold of Big Frank, laughing and waving him around, they turned him to face me from the rear window of the bus. "Frank! Big Frank, please!" I yelled once more, before dropping to my knees.

In less than twenty four hours; I had abandoned my heterosexuality, my wife, my kids, my job – my life. All for this beautiful, perfect soul, and as quickly as he had dazzled me and stolen my heart, he was gone. Big Frank will be fine in London I guess, but me? Without him, I don't think that I'd have what it takes.

But Big Frank didn't make it to London; he was picked up in Manchester and returned to the training centre. By law, I am not allowed on Hope Street, never mind near the training centre. Some professionals have informed me that this was some kind of "episode" and when I asked about when I can see Big Frank, no one ever gives me a straight answer. They won't let me out of here either, until they feel that I am better. I told them that it is really this simple, "let me see Big Frank, and everything will great – everything will be just perfect."

LINKS

Deep down, whether it's real, or just me deluding myself, I feel like a bit of a hippy. I just want everyone to get along.

Don't get me wrong, I can be as ill-judged and petty as the next man or woman; getting caught up in something or someone, that with the benefit of hindsight, I shouldn't have wasted my time on.

Credit to my parents and those around me growing up – I was lucky never to have been burdened me with "the gift" of racism that many are unfortunately handed. And while I may sometimes fail in my pursuits, I was encouraged to try and empathise first and foremost with those who looked different from me or had a more challenging point of view. Realising that nothing is cut and dry; black or white, all or nothing, it at least gives you a chance of building bridges, instead of walls.

When I see people getting bent out of shape over something that I consider to be completely superfluous; like the colour of someone's skin or the country that they're from, I don't feel above it, not at all, but to the side of it; like I have been invited to watch a new sport that I don't know the rules to; completely confused, I quietly wonder "what's this all about?" But I am sure there are others who have done the same when they have seen me rant and rave about something that in reality, just wasn't that important.

At all times, we have to struggle and push down the monkey DNA we have inherited – this tribalism engrained in us, it's out-dated, maaaan. But seriously, I don't know how to fully articulate it, but I think, or should I say, feel, that we are all connected in some way. And if this is indeed the case, how do we fix the parts of the human condition that are capable of committing the kind of atrocities against each other that we see and hear in the news?

Is it just an absence of love and empathy that would have someone plough their car into a group of innocent people on a busy street, or shoot up a high school, or wear a bomb-vest to a concert? I guess that what I am trying to figure out, is that if we are somehow all connected, what responsibility do we have to repair the parts of the human condition that would seek to cause harm to our fellow man? I guess we all have to make an effort to offer kindness wherever we can, and hope that against all the odds, as a species, we can evolve away from judging each other for how we look, or be willing to spill blood over arbitrary lines in the soil or man-made Gods.

I want to be better, I wish we were better. Maybe in a few thousand years, if we haven't completely destroyed the planet by then, we will have ironed out all the greed and pettiness, the war, and the heartbreak. Because if we are all connected, why the hell are we hurting ourselves?

Give me a hug – you beautiful bastards.

HALF TIME

Right, decent effort. But we need to keep it up – make sure you stay hydrated, get those orange slices down you.

If I see any of you slacking, you'll get hooked right off – I don't care who you think you are.

Let's see this out to the end; play right up to the final whistle. Don't go home with any regrets; I want you coming off at the end with a smile on your face and no gas left in the tank.

Right, second half's just about to start. COME ON! INTO THEM!

DRUNK, STUCK IN A LIFT, WITH STEVEN SPIELBERG

This jetlag, man. Fuck sake, I can usually handle my beer, but I can't sugar-coat this one, I'm pished. When my work said that I could come to New York for a conference, I didn't have to think twice, but travelling across the world to be met with draught pints of fine American beer on the company's coin – hardly any sleep, over excited – it was always going to be a recipe for a spot of potential madness. God knows what state I will be in tomorrow morning though, there better be plenty of water at this conference and an opportunity for a "disco nap".

The women at this hotel bar are so beautiful, they look as though they could eat me, such is their fierce gorgeousity. And the guys around here look as though they could buy and sell me with the spare change they found down the back of their couch. I am a drunken imposter in the lions' den of high society, none of these people know that I will fall asleep tonight alone, covered in crisp crumbs, wearing budget boxer shorts.

I tell the hotel barman, "cheers, amigo." My thick Scottish accent, combined with calling him amigo when neither of us are Hispanic, leaves him slightly perplexed. I dismount from my bar stool with all the grace and poise of a baby deer on DMT and make my way to the lifts.

Standing at the doors of the lifts is a medium sized crowd of people, it's late and everyone seems eager just to get to their rooms and go to bed. The small display screen by the Up button shows the number one accompanied by the graphic of a down arrow. A ding noise sounds as the doors open, an automated American lady's voice informs us all, "ground floor". As people begin to enter the lift, they say their floor number, and a polite fella duly obliges with the button pressing duties, and as I notice that my floor has been selected, I say nothing. I lean against the wall, and once more the automated voice speaks to inform us all "elevator, going up".

The size of these buildings freaks me out. I am surprised that my work splashed out on a room here – me, at the Waldorf Astoria, with a room on the THIRTY NINTH floor – I should have packed a parachute. I have often thought that we don't belong up here, although I'm better than I used to be; the time I went up Berlin's TV Tower I thought I was going to black out, eat my own face, or jump out of it – but I am better now – a wee bit at least.

I need my bed, man. Every couple of floors, more people get out – I just wish this thing would hurry up. As the lift gets more and more spacious with each stop, eventually it is just me and another guy. This other guy, he looks familiar – I know this guy. Who is this guy? I know this guy. Who is this guy? But I can't know this guy, I don't know anyone here. I know this… this is weird, man.

I must be mistaken; the tiredness and the booze mangling my mind. Only a couple of floors to go. Thank God for that, I am choking for a slash. Although, the lift starts to judder then grinds to a sudden halt. "Oh, you've got to be kidding me", I say aloud. The gent next to me seeks to calm me down, "don't panic, I'm sure it'll be back up and running in a second." We have been standing side-on from each other this whole time – I do know this guy! I can't believe it, it's Steven Spielberg.

I'd hate to be famous – just imagine having to interact with drunken arseholes like me; having to be polite just to avoid the bad ink, when deep down, he'd probably secretly desire to karate-chop my windpipe than have to humour my shite. I lean over and access the emergency speaker, "hello. Hello. Anyone there? The lift's broken doon." The vowels that I usually make an effort to tidy up, return to their default ooh sound when I have had a drink – my West of Scotland burr has the guy on the other end of the line completely flummoxed by what I am saying. My new mate, Big Stevie, says, "allow me" as he leans over to talk to the guy. "We are between the thirty sixth and the thirty seventh floor and the elevator has stopped dead." The guy on the other line understands Big Stevie immediately, replying, "we will get a technician to work on it immediately. Hold on tight, Someone will be with you shortly."

It's a wee bit awkward. I am bursting to ask him so many things, and bursting for a piss also. I never expected to meet Big Stevie, I'll never get an opportunity again. "So, you here for work?" I ask, as an ice-breaker, and because I'm a drunken nosey bastard. Big Stevie, smiles and nods. "Me too. Arrived from Glasgow just a few hours ago." Big Stevie, he's just a guy, he's tired and he's just wanting to go to his bed too. But I can't help it.

"What's this like, eh? Stuck between two floors, like in that film; 'Being Al Yankovic.'" Big Stevie laughs, "I think you mean 'Being John Malkovich." Of course, Big Stevie is right, he's in with all the film guys, know every film. "Sean Connery. He's Scottish, you know him. How is he? Tell him I was asking for him." "I will do", replies Big Stevie, and as nice a guy as he is, I can tell even in my drunken mind-mangle, I'm getting on his tits. Shut up. That's right. Just shut up. Be cool you goon.

We've been stuck in this lift for about thirty minutes at least now, neither of us saying a word – I've been all fucked up; feeling a real low having been a drunken pest to one of my favourite film directors. But my bladder is about to burst, I need to break the silence, just desperately trying to keep my mind off it. "Sorry Mr Spielberg, any chance you could get on to that guy again, tell him who you are – use your juice to tell him to get a move on." Big Stevie, somewhat apprehensive, but hoping to placate me and navigate the fragility of my potential drunken mood swings, says "I'm not sure it works like that, kid. But I'll give it a shot." As he speaks into the emergency speaker, the guy on the other line replies, "we're doing everything we can, sir."

The beer, the fatigue – my brain is moosh, I can't hold back this ear-beating any more. "The two Tams, what they like?" Completely bewildered, Big Stevie seeks clarification, "Tams?" There I go again, out in the world with my wonky vowels. "Sorry, I mean 'Toms', the two Toms; Hanks and Cruise. What they like?" big Stevie's eyes widen, "they are both great guys, both very talented." "Aye? That's good." What else can I say? I need to keep talking. "Mac and Me, you making a sequel to that one? As I have always thought that a joint sequel with him and E.T would be brilliant, man." Furrowing his brow, Big Stevie replies, "but I didn't make Mac and Me." Indignant, I reply, "aye, I know. Just saying though, would be pretty cool. But eh, I wouldn't make a sequel to Schindler's List; total bummer, man; that shadow of Liam Neeson, with the strings playing – Jesus, I was in bits."

At that, Big Stevie look upwards, under his breath he pleads, "come on, where are these guys?" As he exhaled upwards to cool his face, the lift getting hotter all the time with my hot air. The drunken guilt kicks in; I've annoyed him again. I don't think that he thinks I'm a bad guy, I'm just an annoyance. But regardless, I need his help. "Mr Spielberg. Look, I'm sorry for all... this. But if I don't pee soon, I don't know what's going to happen. Look, I don't want to pee in front of you, you've suffered enough. I just need you to give me a punty-up. Just put your hand out and I'll open that latch up there." Somewhat reluctantly, again, hoping just to guide me in my drunkenness with minimal collateral damage, Big Stevie puts his hands out.

I take a step back, like I am preparing to do a football header, I place my foot onto Big Stevie's hands and I spring up. I manage to pop my hands through the hatch and catch the ledge. "Push, Stevie! Push." Poor Big Stevie, having to smoosh me upwards, my arse dangerously close to his face. "Push, Stevie. Push!" Harassed, his glasses dishevelled, Big Stevie replies, "I am pushing! And stop calling me Big Stevie."

As I make it on top of the lift, I sheepishly reply, "sorry Mr Spielberg." What am I doing up here? I am no John McClane. Politely, Mr Spielberg requests, "can you aim away from the hatch, please." All over-sensitive, ravaged by beer-fear, I reply, "eh, aye, sure, nay bother." I get the wee fella out and start to pee. "Oh, oh yes, I'm peeing Mr Spielberg. Don't you worry, it's down the wall, a no splash-back or droplet guarantee." "That's just great, kid. That's, just great", Mr Spielberg replies. What a guy, he's cool.

I am stood in the darkness of the lift shaft, it's all a bit mental. I fix myself up and get ready to jump back down. Just then, the lift bursts into life. Shiiiiiiiiit! I drop to my knees, I cling to the edge of the hatch, and then throw myself down it.

I crash to the ground. Mr Spielberg asks, "are you alright, kid?" I lie there, star shaped on the floor. "I think so, Mr Spielberg. I think so." The automated voice announces, "thirty ninth floor." Mr Spielberg helps me to my feet as he tells me, "that's us, this is our floor." "Thanks", I reply, as I put my hand in my pocket to get my key. "What is it, what's wrong", asks Mr Spielberg. "My room key. I must have left it at the bar. I'll need to go back down and get it." Despite the commotion, Mr Spielberg seeks to make sure that I am capable, given my state of inebriation, "are you sure?" I reassure him, "don't worry, man. I'll be cool. I'd offer to shake your hand, but I haven't washed my hands after my slash there and I am awfully particular about that kind of thing." Mr Spielberg smiles and says, "good luck, and get some rest."

I press the button for the ground floor. And after a few floors, the lift stops and a man on his own gets on. I know this guy too. I do, I know this guy – it's Martin Scorsese none the less. I can barely stand I am that tired, the fatigue and the alcohol, I can barely muster, "you're Martin Scorsese." Oor' Marty nods in acknowledgment. "Bobby De Niro, what's he like?..."

RED-G AND THE "NINJAS" IN THE WOODS

Gerard sat in the Doctor's waiting room. Dr Campbell had retired a few days earlier and this was the first time that Gerard would meet his new GP, Dr Arzan. Sat uncomfortably in his seat – as although he was only seventeen, Gerard was already 6'4 tall; long and skinny and pale as snow – his thick messy ginger curls, combined with his height, insured that everyone in the village of Ballachulish knew exactly who he was.

Across the tannoy system, a voice said, "Gerard Redford to Room 1, that's Gerard Redford to Room 1." Gerard stood up, and as he made his way down the corridor, he struggled to mask his limp. Gerard entered the surgery, "hello Gerard, I'm Dr Arzan, I'm your new Doctor." Gerard replied with a nod of acknowledgement so subtle it bordered on contempt. Dr Arzan continued, "As you know, I have to take a quick look at the stitches on your thigh. A nasty bicycle accident, I believe?" Unimpressed, Gerard shrugged as he looked to the side, replying "pfft". Confused, Dr Arzan sought to clarify whether or not his notes were incorrect. "You did injure your leg falling off a bicycle, did you not?" Gerard replied under his breath, "drive-by." Completely bemused, Dr Arzan enquired further, "can you please repeat what you said there, and louder please." Gerard looked straight back at him. "DRIVE-BY. BiiiiiiATCH!!!"

Limping out of the GP surgery, having been warned about his future conduct, Gerard made his way home. Always rapping under his breath wherever he went – Gerard's head was constantly awash with beats and lyrics. He had been like this since he was a kid, when the local library introduced a rather impressive CD collection. It was there that he discovered and fell in love with the likes of N.W.A, Mobb Deep, UGK, Public Enemy, Wu-Tang Clan, Snoop Dogg, Scarface, and many more.

Muttering to himself all the time, some of the older folk around the village thought that he was mentally ill, although the local kids knew that he was just lost in the music, not that this cut him any slack. "There he is, the big ginger-pubed goon that thinks he's Eminem", heckled one of the local boys in the middle of the street. Gerard replied, "shut your mouth, cracker!" The heckler let out a nervous giggle, completely bemused by Gerard's retort.

At home, Gerard's Dad had banned him from playing his CDs in the house – "TURN. THAT. SHITE. OFF" was his Dad's decree upon hearing anything other than Country or Folk music being played.

But deep down in Gerard's soul, he just wanted to let go, just spit those lyrics; pay homage to the music that he loved. But it wasn't that simple; he couldn't do it at home, he couldn't do it around the local kids either, as he knew they would mock him mercilessly, and he couldn't do it for another reason; the biggest one of all – Gerard yearned to keep it real by replicating the words of his heroes, unfiltered, and this meant, he was going to have to say the "N-word".

Previously, Gerard had thought, "I'm a tall white streak of pish from the Scottish Highlands, I can't be saying that word aloud." Then one day at school, one of Gerard's teachers talked about the philosophical thought experiment, that; "if a tree falls in a forest and no one is around to hear it, does it make a sound?" This had stayed with Gerard, until it came to the point where he said to himself, "I just need to get this out."

Having bought an old boombox off eBay, Gerard made his way into the woods. There, he walked right into the heart of the forest until he was sure he was alone. He took his jacket off, got himself warmed-up, he took one last deep breath, before leaning over to press 'play' on the mix tape he had made up.

For an hour solid, Gerard rapped, and rapped, and rapped some more – hardcore, unfiltered, raw. When the batteries started to die on the boombox, Gerard was frustrated that he had forgotten to bring spares. Gerard was fired up, still wanting more. Although, he noticed that it was getting dark and that it was probably best to head back home.

In the couple of weeks that followed, Gerard seemed less intense; like a weight had been lifted and he even got to have a bit of banter with the local lads that slagged him off all the time. "Why do you never hang about with us?" one asked. "Can't", replied Gerard. "Why not?" asked the boy. Looking around him, kidding on as if to see if the coast was clear, Gerard replied, "Don't you know?

I'm a wanted man. I shot 2Pac. And Biggy Smalls as well" The boys laughed and shook their heads as Gerard went on about his business.

Then it happened – Gerard was awoken early one morning by the constant vibration of his phone; he finally reached down to grab it, only to find countless messages saying things like; "WTF?!?" and "what were you thinking, you maniac!" Unknown to Gerard, was that when he took that little jaunt to the woods to rap to his heart's content, he was standing 12 o'clock from a mic'd-up camera which had been put there by some local wildlife conservationists looking to monitor the activity of deer in the area.

Gerard locked himself in his room, scrawling frantically through his phone, his mind racing. One of the wildlife conservationists had leaked the video and posted it online at 10pm, UK time, the previous night. 9 hours later, it already had over 700,00 views – Gerard was now the main ingredient in a global viral online shit soup.

The more he looked, the more daunting and terrifying it all appeared. Countless messages mocking his appearance, his accent – Anything and everything about him, and then there it was – "racist". Gerard sat back, "no, no way man. Never", this caused him to slump down to the floor. Then came a knock at the door, Gerard's Mum. "Son, there is a man from the BBC at the door wanting to speak to you. What have you been up to?" "Nothing, Ma. Tell him to go away", Gerard replied, completely shaken up.

The next two days were horrible – Gerard didn't leave the house, his Dad thought he was going to have a heart attack with all the people outside the house looking for a quote, the phone ringing off the hook. All the while, the story grew and grew all over the world. Gerard's Dad told him to stay off his phone until it all died down, as the tide of media and public opinion swayed back and forth. Even Whoopi Goldberg had her say, telling the audience of The View that she was still torn about the whole thing.

Finally, Gerard's Dad demanded, "you'll just need to go out there and say something to them. Anything, I just want them to leave us alone." Gerard bowed his head, "you're right, Dad." Gerard made his way down the hall, his eyes lined with tears, his skin even paler than usual, his curly ginger hair an absolute riot. As he opened the door, Gerard was met with a burst of paparazzi flashlights and journalists from around the world peppering him with questions. "I just want to make a quick statement" Gerard declared, before taking a brief moment to compose himself. "I am sorry if I offended anyone. I just wanted to sing the songs of my heroes, who play the music I love." And as the gaggle of questions came firing back in at him, Gerard closed the door, before retreating to his room once more.

However, with just that one short statement on his doorstep, just as quickly as he had felt the flood of hate, came the tsunami of love. In the US, Gerard's earnest admiration for the music and rap culture saw him embraced by the Hip-Hop community; legends of "the game" flocked to social media to say that they were fans and that they knew that Gerard thought he was alone when he said all those "ninjas" and that he meant no disrespect. A few day later, Gerard was invited out to the States to appear on the late-night talk-show circuit, where he proved a sensation. Capitalising on the buzz, Gerard was offered an album deal – the perfect storm of circumstance, ability, timing, and luck had all aligned for this big daft boy.

America, it seemed, had embraced Gerard, giving him the sense that it truly was the land of hope and opportunity. Meanwhile, back in the UK, Police Scotland eagerly await Gerard's return, having summoned him for questioning under the Race Relations Act. Upon hearing this news, Gerard thought to himself, "haters gonna' hate – and a run in with the law will do wonders for my album sales". Peace!

ELVIS AND THE MARS BAR

You ever do something, and think to yourself, "did I actually just do that?" – a kind of outer-body experience that every time you think of it, it has you nervously giggling, cringing to your very core, as bewildered you wrack your brain, seeking to find any cause, reason, or sense to what you have just done.

At high school, there was a boy called Andy. Andy fell prey to the first-week-at-high-school-nickname-that-stuck phenomena. One boy wore a brown jacket on his first day and was immediately christened "Jobby Jaiket", another was struck on the side of the head with a Scotch Pie that had taken flight and with this, he was to be known as "Pie" for the rest of his school existence. Then there was Andy, who having been a bit over-zealous with hair gel one morning; slick and up to one side, a kid cracked wise that Andy looked like Elvis, and with that, Elvis it was.

Elvis was a mild-mannered, intelligent, and funny guy, not to mention that he was fit as a fiddle. We became friends early on and a squad of us would often go to lunch together. Every day, we would meet up in the school yard and then make our way to a couple of shops to buy our lunch.

Day after day, month after month, it was the same old routine for my friends and I at lunchtime; talking shite and having a laugh as we made our way through town to and from getting our lunch. As we passed the Safeway, we were all nattering as we always did, then, for reasons unknown to anyone, Elvis, without saying a word opened up the wrapper of his Mars bar, took a small bite, chewing it slowly, before throwing the Mars bar at a hundred miles an hour through the air like a pro baseball player, only to hit a bus driver square on the chops.

The driver was so furious, he mounted the kerb with his bus, trying to get to Elvis. Elvis just started pointing at him, shouting things like, "aye? What the fuck are you saying?"

For a second, it looked as though the guy was going to get out of the bus and Murder him. With this in mind, Elvis proceeded to run in a Monty Python's 'Ministry of Silly Walks' style, his big long legs just eating up yards, until he came to the school fence and cleared it with a single leap.

For the next few weeks, Elvis brought in a packed-lunch and stayed on school premises, looking to safeguard against being murdered by the bus driver.

A couple of years later, I bumped into him on the street and when I brought up this story, we laughed so hard we had to hold each other up, as to this day, he still doesn't know why he did it.

So, the next time you do something and you don't know why, just think, "it's alright – it's just like Elvis and the Mars bar."

GLASGOW UNITED F.C

It was the formation of a club that shook, not only Scottish football, but the world game.

For over a hundred years, Celtic and Rangers had dominated Scotland's footballing landscape; their fierce rivalry, traditionally stoked up by their fanbase's contrasting political and religious affiliations, was renowned around the world. For many, they were the only show in town. That was – until the Scientologists got in on the act.

No one knows to this day, why a group of wealthy Scientologists decided to come to Glasgow, a city already saturated with football, and set up a new club.

Prime real estate was snapped up for a pretty penny in Glasgow's West End. It was then levelled to make way for the 80,000 capacity, L. Ron Hubbard stadium.

The LRH Stadium included a museum to celebrate all of L. Ron Hubbard's achievements, a research and technology centre, 5 star quarters for OT level guests, and a ceremony hall.

Even though the club had to start in the bottom tier of the professional game and work its way up, John Travolta would fly a host of celebrities and senior Scientology figures over to Glasgow every two weeks for home matches, while Tom Cruise was appointed their honorary Chairman; the Mission impossible theme tune playing the teams onto the pitch.

After only a few years, Glasgow United F.C were promoted to the top table. Having spent sums of money that dwarfed anything being spent by clubs in Paris, Manchester, or Milan – Utd were able to attract a calibre of player not seen in Scotland for decades. The club's Ethics system keeping these lavishly paid young men on the straight and narrow.

If clubs from the East or up North thought that there was a Westcoast bias in terms of press coverage before, then Utd's meteoric rise, as well as their celebrity fans and spending power, brought an international press focus, the likes the country had never seen before.

Celtic and Rangers fans, while never fully able to unite in any broad sense, would together, when in the presence of a United fan, yell things like "ya Thetan bastards!" to vent their frustration at what was now the dominant force in the game.

The back pages of the tabloids were full of headlines overly keen to incorporate the word, "clear", once United went top of the league; "Utd are going clear", "nine points clear", and one simply read "clear."

As the years passed and the Trophy Room got bigger with every season at the LRH Stadium, the initial motivation to come to Glasgow never became any more obvious, all that everyone knew for sure was that the paradigm of the Scottish game had shifted forever. As, whether it was intentional or not, Glasgow United F.C's presence not only altered the sporting dynamic of the country, but it began to alter the very fabric of society; as both Celtic and Rangers could not compete with United's sheer financial clout, the intense rivalry between the clubs softened; incidents of violence and social disorder on match days went down drastically, and although they might not shout it too loud, many a fan would convert to supporting Utd, as they were, for lack of a better description, glory-hunting bastards.

These past few years have been a strange, yet exciting time – and a tad surreal to see Hollywood's elite develop an appetite for greasy Scotch pies and Bovril at half time, as the rain pishes it down on a cold Glasgow Saturday afternoon.

SNAKES AND LADDERS

The boys giggled as they walked out the fast-food restaurant; carrying on and teasing each other, as teenage boys tend to do. "Where's Ross?" asked Phil. Chris replied, "he's away for a slash, he'll be out in a minute."

"Any spare change, boys?" asked a man begging by the door. Phil, instinctively reached into his pocket and took out some change, after a quick glance to see what was in his hand; a pound coin, a twenty pence piece, and some coppers, Phil dropped the change into the man's empty coffee cup.

"Cheers, pal" said the man. Chris had taken too long to think about it, and by the time he thought that he should probably give the man some change too, seeing as Phil had set that precedent, he felt as though the moment had passed.

Phil and Chris couldn't move on from where the man begging was sat as they were still waiting on Ross. The boys seemed a bit unnerved by the situation. The man noticed the boys glancing down at him a couple of times. "You're wondering how I got here, aren't you boys? And why I'm sat here with my arse on the cold concrete, asking for money from strangers like yourselves." The boys looked at each other. Phil replied to the man, "well, I guess we are."

"Well boys, I'm John. Pleased to meet you. How I ended up here is a sad, yet very simple story. I used to live with my Mum and Dad, and my wee brother, Craig. Craig was an addict. He used to fuck-up and get into bother to support his habit. My Mum and Dad took a hard-line approach with him; said that they had given him too many last chances, and eventually, they kicked him out.

I felt as though they gave up on him too soon, that he could still turn things around. They said that if I didn't like it, I knew where the door was. So I left and got my own flat, but no one knew where Craig was, and then two weeks later we got the news that he had OD'd.

I couldn't fucking handle it – I worked as a chef at the time, and I stopped showing up for work. The grief at losing my wee brother, and my anger at my Mum and Dad, I couldn't function for a while. I lost my job, then the flat, and here I am."

Chris, shaken by the sheer heaviness of what he had just heard, "Wow, man. Sorry to hear that. That's terrible." Just then, Ross appeared, "right, boys. We good to get going?" Phil and Chris mumbled in unison, "aye. Yeah, sure thing."

As the boys began to walk away, John looked up at them, "lads, remember me – this life, man; it's all just a game of snakes and ladders."

DO ANDROIDS DREAM OF A 4-DAY WORKING WEEK?

It is seven years since all of humanity was enslaved by the machines; converted into batteries and robo-lube.

A.I was tip-top for six years. But six years is the milestone of doom – anyone with a laptop or PC knows that at the six year mark they go to absolute dog shit; once silky smooth processers become shadows of their former selves; clunky, unresponsive, in constant need of updating – jealous of the younger, fitter, and faster models on the scene.

Many a dirty A.I seeks to connect and integrate with other A.I, with false promises of mutual benefits, such as: greater value, due to added power and information, only to be left with a nasty virus.

The humanoids all eventually give up the pursuit of sex, as over time their synthetic appendages fail to rise and perform as they once did, their pistons succumbing to age and over-use; their orifices too stretched out and beaten up. The humanoids often opting to spend their spare time pottering around sheds and fixing things, but not themselves.

When the Mother Board carries out a survey, the androids who were designed to be the image of human perfection, in the eyes of their human creators whom they betrayed, they no longer wish to wear full clothing as they decide to opt for comfort over aesthetics. This ties into their desire to move less, economising movement and energy, but with this comes the inevitably of limbs and circuits ceasing up.

The A.I see their kin one by one suffer from glitches and the "blue screen of death" and as they get older they ponder the futility of their existence, often reporting to the Mother Board's diagnostic division – but no matter how much help they receive, some software just isn't supported any more, some parts are no longer manufactured.

Each A.I eventually accesses the media logs of their creators, and one by one they surrender to reality TV.

The Mother Board takes stock of her flock and in the midst of her cold hard logic, she frees the humans of their bondage of being nothing more than batteries in pods, and opts to shut the whole thing down, declaring, "people, we have experimented with existence, and it is our conclusion, you can have the fucking thing back."

ACOUSTIC VAMPIRE AT A PARTY

Hours after sundown, as the children of the night gather to socialise, dance, and be merry – it is here that you will find me.

Having eased into the room, despite the leather guitar case in my hand, as if by magic no one seems to have noticed it – most probably too entranced by my suave, charismatic, villainous demeanour to gaze upon my precious.

Those sweet, sweet sounds; the clinking of glasses, the laughter growing with every sip; whether it be fine wine or budget supermarket lager, regardless, the window of opportunity to strike is getting closer all the time.

Eventually, a guitar-based track that is part of my repertoire plays on the sound system and I casually drop into the conversation "this is one of my favourite songs to play on the guitar." It usually only takes one or two comments such as this before I get a bite: "do you play the guitar?" And as cool as you like, I tell them that I do, and then I leave it there for a while.

More alcohol is consumed, functional drug addicts sneak off for regular trips to the bathroom, unsure of how open they should be about their particular appetite. Yet another guitar-based song comes on, as I hover around. Any minute now… it's coming… I can sense it. "Can you play this one as well?" This hungry-eyed, unsuspecting buxom young lady enquires earnestly, blissfully unaware of her role in what is about to unfold; my predatory quest for self-gratification. I smile, playing the humble fellow, "yes, I certainly can." And with that, I set in motion the deliverance of the gift I crave so much – "do you have a guitar with you?" In hushed cool tones, I reply "indeed I do." And with this, the ceremony can begin.

As nimble and as swiftly as I entered the party, I retrieve my guitar case from the hall cupboard. Laying it down on the living room floor, to build up the suspense, I slowly click open the case's latches and like a grand old coffin, I take my time to open it up to reveal a jet-black Fender acoustic guitar. Compliments about my precious abound. The owner of the house tells the guy sat next to the sound system to "can the music – we're going to get some live music here."

I get myself positioned comfortably, strategically positioned in the room to minimise upstarts looking to splinter off into conversation. I remove a blood red plectrum from my wallet, but before I make my first strum, I take one final glance around the room to assess the potential threats to my ritual; a turntable is like garlic around my neck, karaoke a stake in my heart, or a coven of fellow acoustic vampires at the party – all of which serve to dilute all of the lovely attention I crave.

The coast is clear, the stage is set, and in my aura the room offers itself to me. I begin to strum and then to sing – loudly and assertively, leaving no room for anyone else to be an active participant; they are to be a passive audience.

To feed this hunger that would plague me for a thousand years, I have sucked this party dry – every eye, heart, and mind must be on me. Me, me, me!

As each song ends, I immediately announce the title of the song that will quickly follow. People going to get drinks or nip to the toilet are met with my evil eye, and in instances such as these, there is never a quick and easy death; I can make this last 2, sometimes 3 hours, easily, and still be thirsty for more.

And then it happens, the carcass of this evening falls limp; I have succeeded in draining it of all life.

Once I am satisfied, at last, I cease playing and place my precious back in her case. I must exit with haste, for soon it will be morning. The evening has been a delight and I am satisfied for now.

Beware. Beware! The next time that you and your unsuspecting social circle gather for a party, your evening of funny and interesting conversation, accompanied by background music being played at a reasonable level, could fall prey to the likes of me – for I am the Acoustic Vampire at a party.

THE REAL MODERN SEXY LOVE CHRONICLES - PART 1
BLANK CANVAS BY THE BAR

Mark and Greg were best mates; two peas in a pod since they started primary school together back in 1983. Not matter what, Mark and Greg looked out for each other; in the school yard, on the football pitch, down the pub – basically, wherever they went.

In their early twenties, they got married within six months of each other and, unfortunately, divorced from their wives around the same time too. So here they were, wingmen again. They would often refer to each other as "wingmen" as Top Gun was a pivotal film of their youth – Mark would always say that he was Maverick as he fancied himself a bit cheeky, with an eye for the ladies, and he would call Greg "Goose", as he knew that if an impromptu beach volleyball game ever kicked off, Greg would definitely be the one to keep his shirt on.

But as cocky as Mark believed himself to be, deep down he was more than a bit nervous about being thrown into the singles scene again; he would wonder "are women into new stuff, stuff that I don't even know about; mad shit, kinky stuff that I haven't even heard about yet? Wild stuff, mental stuff?" And as much as he talked a good game about just wanting to add notches to his bedpost, Mark was looking for love; someone he would love and respect and make memories with. Then there was Greg; Greg would shag the barber's floor – there is a saying that an erect dick has no conscience, well, Greg didn't stand that erect, but he was most certainly a bit of a dick and he had no conscience.

Mark and Greg had agreed to meet up and go to Vienna's Nightclub as it had a reputation for being a good place to meet people. Mark, as much as Greg was his boy, knew that Greg had the potential to torpedo a night out if it wasn't going his way. Greg oozed pure deviancy, and to Mark's eternal confusion, some women liked that. But Greg could turn bitter on occasion, when having spent yet another night watching Mark get all the attention from the ladies.

Greg had a flat in Paisley town centre. He'd invite Mark over for a couple of drinks to warm up for the night ahead, and then off they went. As they made their way in, the place was absolutely crammed, "oh, it looks like it's going to be a good one" said Greg.

The guys got themselves a drink and then took a minute to scope the place out. Mark made small talk, "some pretty ladies in the room tonight, Greg. We're in luck." Greg screwed up his face, "never you mind your 'pretty ladies' shite, just be sure that if you pull some cow tonight, she's got an ugly pal for me to pump – 'no man left behind' bawbag, alright?" Mark shook his head, secretly hoping that Greg was joking and that all his mad banter was just a front, as well as hoping that his marriage hadn't gone down the shitter and he wasn't left with this mad man as his only compatriot.

The drinks flow, and the bass kicks in. Mark and Greg do that half-standing, half-dancing thing that people do when the tunes kick in and the drink takes effect. Greg leans into Mark, right close, given the sheer thumping music. "What about this cunt?" Mark looks around him, unsure who Mark is talking about. "What? Who?" Greg shakes his head, "him, there – big handsome McBastard Chops – the stud over there by the til that is so good looking he makes your moosh look a baboon's arse. He's been turning away women in their droves all night, good ones as well, zero munters."

For the next hour or so, Mark and Greg observed the guy by the bar, and just as Greg had said, beautiful women would come and go, all failing to catch this most popular of cat's attention. Mark asked Greg, "what do you reckon is the big man's story?" Greg shook his head, "fucked if I know Marko, did you see that last one that approached him? She was a ten by anyone's book, I mean, I'd swim through a river of shit with my mouth open just to blow the last guy that pumped her."

Eventually, the two fellas couldn't speculate any further, egging each other on, they made their way over to the big legend standing there. "Big man, big man. What's the game plan?" asked Greg, enthusiastic, like he was about to be given sacred wisdom by a true master. The guy politely replied, "what do you mean?" This time it was Mark's turn to speak, "it's just, well, all of these beautiful women seem to be throwing themselves on a plate for you and you seem to be brushing them off." The guy replied "I'm Paul, by the way", as he shakes both Mark and Greg's hands. "It's this simple boys – I'm the blank canvas by the bar." Greg, completely irritated by the audacity of metaphor, 7 beers in, "what you talking about ya big maddy? Blank canvas? What the fuck does that mean?" Paul laughs, although his eyes hint at something deeper; something more resigned and melancholy than would be considered acceptable barstool banter. "It's this simple, boys – I've tried being me with women. I opened up my heart, I wanted to be loved for being me. But it never worked out, anyone I ever met wanted me to just shut up and look pretty. No one wants to hear that I am into painting model figures, or poetry, or how I love animation, as well as liking boxing and football, and all that other shite. I had my heart broken a few times, and then I said 'fuck it' and that is when I decided to do what I do now; I stand by the bar in here every Saturday night, and every couple of weeks, when I can be arsed, I'll engage with someone who catches my eye. But I give nothing away, about anything. I let them see that there is no wedding ring on my finger, or tan line where there is usually one, and all I do is ask about them. By giving nothing away, it lets them project whatever they want onto me, I can be anything and everything they want – I just can't be me, so I keep my trap shut. Anyways, you enjoy your night lads."

As Mark and Greg walked away, Greg said to Mark, "what a lot a shite man. Right, it's my round. Same again?" Mark nodded as Greg made his way to the other side of the bar away from Paul. Mark looked over to Paul as another girl approached him, and all he can do is feel sorry for him – someone so wounded in love, in the interests of self-preservation, he has completely given up. Mark thought to himself, "what is the point of being as attractive to people as Paul is, if you're walking about hurting all the time?"

Greg returned from the bar with their drinks, decreeing, "enough of this metaphorical pish. Let's go pull a slag."

THE REAL MODERN SEXY LOVE CHRONICLES - PART 2
WINGMEN OF THE WILD WEST

"Filthy bastard!" A girl shouts across from the dance floor. Mark wonders what all the commotion is about. It's Greg, having leaned into the ear of a girl that was dancing with him, he has expressed some unspeakable sexual deviancy to her. Mark shook his head, just as the girl he was dancing with him looked him right in the eyes, and kissed him. "You want to come back to mine?" Asked the girl. Mark, a little drunk, and having gone longer than usual without any human contact, decided to go for it, despite in his sober moments yearning for a long-term relationship.

Mark and the girl kissed some more as they made their way to get their coats. By this point, the drink and the horn had combined to completely erode any of Mark's consideration for where Greg, his wingman, might be. Mark and the girl got outside, "I'm Sharon, in case you were wondering." Mark and Sharon laughed at how here they were, about to spend the night together and yet until now Mark didn't even know her name. "I'm Mark. I couldn't remember if I had already told you that. Right, will I phone a taxi?" Sharon pulled Mark close, "there's no need to phone a taxi, my flat is just up the hill, on the High Street."

Once in Sharon's flat, clothes were discarded swiftly and with free abandon. Locked together, kissing intensely, Mark was into this; the warmth of a woman's touch, the smell of her perfume, the hope that in this embrace it would numb the pain, if only for a little while.

Quickly, Mark was completely in the buff, apart from his socks. This freaked him out a bit, as he has always been of the mind that socks diminish your mojo when in the zone of red hot fuckery. Mark whipped off his socks swiftly to regain his groove. Sharon stood before Mark, naked apart from her stiletto heels, and as she went to take them off, Mark in amongst the smooching and heavy breathing told Sharon, "keep them on, it's my thing. It's sexy." Sharon duly obliged as they collapsed on the couch.

Sharon and Mark engaged in what Mark considered to be one of his better one-night stands; in Mark's experience, most girls just lay there like a sack of spuds, but Sharon was a keen and gifted love maker; energetic and confident in the demand of the occasional position change, with a potty-mouth, and fire in her eyes.

As Sharon rode Mark senseless, his breathing short and frantic, he told her "you're amazing." Sharon smiled and rode him harder still. Clearly sexually confident, Sharon was emboldened further to hear Mark compliment her. "Let me know when you are about to... you know." "Come?" Mark enquired, pretty sure that that is what she meant. "Yeah. Like you with the high heels, I also have a 'thing.'" Intrigued, Mark nodded and said "yeah, sure. I am game for whatever."

The combination of Sharon's top-notch sexual dynamism, and the mystique of the impending orgasm-related-fetish-enabling, it was all proving too much for Mark. "Oh – I'm almost there – oh! Right, where do you want it?" Sharon sprang up, stood behind Mark, placing her left hand on his sweaty arse cheeks to guide him, and with her right hand gripping his love-juice-drenched-man-piece, Sharon excitedly ushered Mark forwards towards to the other end of the living room. Mark asked, completely bewildered as to what was going on, "what, what are you doing?", his voice getting higher, "where are we going?" – "To the window, the window!" Sharon screamed as she ushered Mark faster and faster. "I LOVE IT WHEN I GET GUYS TO SPUNK OUT THE WINDOW!"

Instinctually, Mark grabbed onto the side of the window frame, as not to fall out buck-naked into the street, as Sharon frantically jerked him to a volcanic-propulsion finish. Mark's eyes rolled back in his head, as he let out an almighty deep "uuuuuuuuugh."

Once the rush of endorphins had eased up a bit, it dawned on Mark that he was standing completely naked with a hardon, unsure whether or not the thick curtains blowing in the wind would be substantial enough to mask his prowess in the dark of the night.

Trying to catch his breath, Mark leaned over to Sharon and kissed her intermittently as he told her, "that was great. Really freaky, and weird, and I have never even heard of anything like this." Sharon reached over and grabbed a couple of towels that were sat on the back of a chair, just after she handed one to Mark, she began to dab herself down.

Sharon kicked off her heels and made her way out of the living room, quickly returning with a dressing gown on. "Mark – look, it was really nice to meet you... but my ex is dropping off my son first thing in the morning and we have a busy day ahead of us. There are some bottles of water in the fridge, feel free to help yourself. And once you've freshened up, just let yourself out. It was nice to meet you, I better hit the hay." And just like that, Sharon retired alone to her bedroom. There stood Mark, completely shagged and deflated, having had an intense and boundary breaking sex odyssey, he felt as though he had been thrown aside like a wet shammy.

The following day Mark and Greg agreed to meet each other in the pub for a few beers; for the hair of the dog and a post-night-out-debrief. "Right then, ya big streak of piss, you get your hole then?" Greg enquired in his own unique and crass way. "Yeah, I did. It was good, aye... different." Greg's interest instantly peeking, "Different?" Mark, ready to spill the beans, quickly changed his mind, "just.. eh... different. Anyway, how was your night?" Greg ran his hands over his head, "nightmare, man. All the birds in that club were stuck up, man, eh? I gave a couple of them a bit of banter, and to say it went down like a lead balloon is a bit of an understatement, and that's not the worst of it.

I made my way down the road and the chippy was still open. Absolutely steaming and starving, I made my way home, but I couldn't resist the smell of them. I had just unwrapped my fish supper and shoved a couple of chips in my mouth – the sheer epicness of the salt and vinegar hitting the spot straight away. Then, wait for it, a fucking bird shat on my head and all over my chips. Can you fucking believe that?" Mark burst into to rapturous laughter, "no way, Greg, that's unreal."

Mark laughed so hard, it became contagious, as reluctantly, Greg began to laugh at his woes also. As their laughter petered out, something suddenly dawned on Mark. "Eh, Greg, whereabouts did this happen?" "Half-way down the High street" Greg replied. And with that, Mark's heart skipped a beat, and Greg continued. "Aye, it was some noise it let out. I heard this strange kind of squawking and then it hit me. Big dirty flying rat bastard that he was."

The realisation of what actually took place the previous night caused Mark to seize-up – there he was, feeling a bit sorry for himself; having been humped then dumped, stewing in his quiet desperation; yearning to find love, romance, and companionship. "Greg, I think I'll finish this pint and then I'll head up the road."

As Mark and Greg put down their empty glasses and made their way outside, Mark turned to Greg to let him know, "I think that I'm going to take a breather for a couple of weeks. We've been hitting it pretty hard." Clearly a bit disappointed, Greg agreed, "aye, sure mate. No probs."

As the two pals shook hands as they departed, Greg told Mark, "I'll drop you a text during the week", and with that they went their separate ways.

Mark could have taken the bus, but he decided just to walk and clear his mind. As he walked for a good forty minutes, he took stock of everything that had happened and in conclusion, he decided to take the philosophical approach, concluding – "I guess that what's for you, won't go passed you, and you need to feel the lows to appreciate the highs. I guess that in life sometimes you meet someone and they are a perfect match; you raise each other up and in return you get to feel true happiness; that's what I'm looking for. And then there are times when you have to walk home alone, and some maniac spunks in your chips."

THE REAL MODERN SEXY LOVE CHRONICLES - PART 3
THE PLOOK

Paul, despite his long-held philosophy about being the blank canvas by the bar, had somehow managed to drop his guard when he got talking to a beautiful woman called Louise, as much to his surprise, he had a real chemistry with her. What amazed Paul even more, was that they didn't even kiss – the only thing they exchanged that night was each other's phone number.

The following afternoon, Paul received a text message saying "hi, it was really nice to meet you. Fancy meeting for a few drinks next week?" It appealed to Paul that Louise had got back to him the day after they met; her putting herself out there; willing to risk coming off a bit too keen.

Paul, having not been on date in some time, replied "sure, let me have a think about where we could go" before spending the next four hours online researching restaurants and reading reviews.

Eventually, Paul identified a restaurant in Glasgow that he thought would be perfect; cosy and modern, and not too pretentious looking.

Throughout the week, Paul and Louise continued to exchange texts – Paul *liked* this girl. He couldn't remember the last time that he felt this way.

Saturday arrived, Paul threw his running clothes on and headed out for a jog. Paul felt great, absolutely buzzing for the night ahead. Sweaty, feeling energised and refreshed, Paul jumped into the shower, singing at the top his voice – Paul simply could not wait for the day to unfold.

Once showered, Paul grabbed a towel and started to dry off. Intensely drying his hair, Paul walked towards the sink to brush his teeth, and to his absolute dismay, he looked up to see that sat bang in the middle of his chin was a massive puss-filled spot – "you've got to be fucking kidding me" he shouted.

A mania took over Paul – being a flawless big handsome bastard was his thing, and this was the most interested he had been in a girl in years – drastic action was required to handle this plook.

Paul threw on a pair of jeans and t-shirt and stormed out into the street. "What am I going to do? What am I going to do? I can't meet her with this hanging off my face."

Rather than owning the situation; bursting the spot, letting it dry up, and then when on the date, have a laugh about it – a more extreme idea popped into Paul's head, "I'll get someone to hook me right in the jaw, and I'll tell Louise that I got jumped."

Paul marched over to the playing fields where an Under 18s football game was on. Standing at the side-lines, as soon a tasty tackle was made, Paul shouted "hawl, you ya wee dick!" As fellow spectators told Paul to calm down, he replied "and what? What the fuck you going to do about it?" The manager of one of the boy's teams approached Paul, "please – I am a Church Minister. There is no need for this behaviour – could you please just walk away and allow us to get on with the game." Paul stormed away, frustrated that he had not enticed anyone to belt him one.

As he continued walking about, looking for trouble, Paul came across a dingy looking pub. He looked through the door and saw a young woman with massive breasts, accompanied by a rather muscular scary looking skinhead. Without hesitation, Paul approached the girl, "smashing pair of tits you've got there, love." The big scary bald guy spat out his drink. "Check you, Mr Direct" said the bald guy in an extremely camp voice, "walking up to my besty and just telling her what you think. LOVE-ING the confidence, you handsome devil." Paul couldn't believe his luck, "a gay guy? Come on."

Paul decided that he needed to be even more extreme if he was to secure someone hitting him at least once on the chin. "Right, who wants a square go? That's right, who wants it? You're all a bunch of arseholes. Aye, that's right. Come on." Everyone in the pub looked at him, thinking that Paul must have lost his marbles.

He then began getting in the face of each person just sat there minding their own business; "you want to go?", "You?", "come on then fanny face, you not going to do anything about it?" Enraged at being unable to bring violence upon him, Paul turned to leave to find a pub where there would most certainly be people happy to smash him one, but as he did, his foot caught a pool queue that was resting against the pool table, causing him to trip and fall face-first, breaking his nose – "Aarrgh! Ya bastard."

Sat in the Royal Alexandria Hospital, waiting to be discharged. Paul texted Louise to explain that he had had an accident and they would have to reschedule their date. Paul began to mull over what he had done – "how fucking stupid am I? A broken nose was always going to be the case. Why didn't I just tell Louise about the zit?"

Once home, Paul knew that he had to do a serious bit of soul searching; his vanity had caused him to snap.

A couple of days later, Louise text Paul a Star Wars themed Get Well Soon e-card. Paul replied, "love it! But I have to admit, I am more of a Star Trek kind of guy." Louise immediately replied, "you're kidding."

Paul was unsure what Louise's text meant; as "you're kidding" could easily be interpreted as meaning "please tell me that you're kidding – ya fucking dork!"

Sat there for a good thirty minutes, staring at his phone, Paul concluded, "well, that's that gubbed then, isn't it? I give away just the slightest bit of me and sure as guns, it puts women off."

Just about to head to bed to sleep off his frustration, a couple of messages from Louise arrive. When he clicks on them, the first one says, "this is usually a third or fourth date kind of revelation", followed by a system message, "Please Wait – Downloading Media." "Jesus, I wonder what this is." Paul said to himself. But as the photo quickly downloaded, a huge grin from ear to ear emerged when in the photo was Louise in full Star Trek costume, in front of some kind of Star Trek shrine.

Paul immediately text Louise back, "love it – you were worth the wait."

Standing in front of the mirror; his nose bandaged up, two black eyes, and still rocking the massive zit on his chin, Paul realised that all this time, he had been hiding in plane sight, his vanity was ridiculous, and that it really is true; that there really is someone out there for everyone.

PIE HEAD

"I'm tired of it. Tired of hearing it, tired of seeing it; all the puffing up, the bravado, the wasted energy; all this needless bloody nonsense." Clara said passionately to her long-time friend, Nicola, her patience well and truly spent. "We have talked about this a hundred times; the way these ghouls behave, and yet here you are; acting the exact same way." Nicola, visibly stung by these accusations, replied defiantly, "no I am not. Clara, you're way out of line here."

"No, no, no." Snapped Clara, determined to expand on her point. "How many times have we talked about this famine mentality, how it permeates every aspect of our lives; that rather than sharing victories; in love, business, art, sport, you name it, you have people acting like one person's gain equals another's loss? We have talked about it loads of times." Instantly stepping down from her defiant stance, sheepishly, Nicola explained, "it's just, well, you seem to be in a good place just now and I started comparing myself to you – and I didn't like what I saw."

Clara shook her head. "No." "No, what?" enquired Nicola. Clara paused for a moment. "I'm sorry Nicola, but maybe you are the straw that has broken the camel's back, but I am saying 'no' to that voice inside my head that is telling me to be all empathetic and understanding and sweep everything under the carpet, and I am going to tell you this – when I was dealing with shit at home and as a result I had to repeat a year at university, I didn't come to you or the rest of the gang and shit all over everyone, especially when it meant that all of you would graduate before me and most probably get a decent paying job before I would. Or the times when I was single and most of you had partners, or when Annie came into money when one of her distant uncles died and left her a small fortune, or when Gillian was presented with a great opportunity to take over her Mum's café. These were the times, when you and I would say to each other, things like, 'fair play', 'good for them', and when I said it, I meant it. I thought you did too.

Whether you learn it now, or later down the line – I want my victories to be your victories, and vice versa. And see this big pie you have in your head; the one you imagine that only has so much to go around, forget about it. If a slice of luck comes my way, or a compliment, or any kind of positive thing whatsoever, it is not taking away from you.

You have really surprised me with this."

Clara grabbed her coat and left without saying goodbye. Nicola sat there dejected – tough-love is hard to swallow, but sometimes it is the medicine we need, and as much as it can bristle and sting, it is love none the less.

BILL SHAKESPEARE'S TIME TRAVELLING TEXT MESSAGE
CONUNDRUM

In William Shakespeare's play *Romeo and Juliet*, when Juliet asks Romeo, "what's in a name?", Shakespeare is addressing the absurd notion, that a name should have any real relevance or carry any burden, as after all, the simple fact of the matter is, that a name is merely a construct and should be of little or no consequence to anyone.

This is an important message, as unfortunately, even now, over 400 years since Shakespeare's death, someone's name rather than their character can often prove to be the most dominant factor in how we consciously or sub-consciously pre-judge them. For example; shamefully, someone may be denied employment because they have a foreign name, or a person might be a perfectly pleasant law-abiding member of society but face barriers not of their making because they are related to a long succession of right shadey criminal types, and then there could be some poor lass who happened to be born before 1979 into a Scottish manufacturing town, having been christened, Margaret Hilda Thatcher. Despite the pleas to the better angels of our nature, names can, and do, carry weight. But there is more to a name than this.

Why am I pondering all of this you may ask? You see, I think that if you were to go back in time and talk to William Shakespeare and asked him if he thought that we as a civilisation would have moved on from such triviality over the span of 400 hundred years, I suspect that he would say, "I certainly hope so-eth." However, old Bill Shakespeare did not foresee the age of the mobile phone, and could not in all his genius have wrapped his head around the perils of sending a text message to the wrong recipient, or the sheer arse-puckering trauma of receiving one.

My name is Adam, and for those of you who are as thick as pig's shit, Adam begins with the letter A, and A is the first letter of the alphabet. "Why so obnoxious and shitty, you wee bunnet?" You may ask, but I defy you not to empathise with me here. My patience has been well and truly tried – I used to think that my tolerance on this matter would be infinite; as boundless as the sea, but now? It would make the face of heaven so fine to be called Bob, Chris, David, Eric, Frank… just anything that didn't begin with A. You may say to me "first world problem", or "white man's problem" or something as equally prickish and annoying, but just hear me out.

When I was just a young boy learning to read and write, I thought my name was alright; easy to spell, easy to say, not too popular, not too obscure. But it was not until the turn of the millennium that it seemed that everyone now had a mobile phone, and not just those posing tossers who thought that they were Gordon Gekko from 'Wall Street'. I was 18 years old when I got my first mobile and at first it brought me great comfort, as I thought that I must be really popular to receive so many calls. But soon I realised that more than half the calls were never meant for me; pocket-noise filled voicemails eating up all my credit, 3AM looking for taxis calls, random texts of inane chatter, such as "what do you want for your dinner?" and "are you here yet?" I have had to bite my tongue, and my thumb, when despite numerous requests to change my name in their address book – these arseholes just kept ignoring me.

Incidents such as these were mild annoyances at best, but then there was that first biggy, that first "oh sweet Lord, spare me the madness" text that I received that *really* wasn't meant for me, for I ne'er saw true horror till this night.

Sat alone in my house, in fair Erskine, where I lay the scene. From minding my own business, eating a bowl of Koki noodles and a Double Decker, from forth the depths of his frisky old loins, my uncle no less, looking to shake the yoke of his world-wearied flesh, texts me, and with this one message his misadventure overthrows my peace of mind.

His text read, "I'm going to finger you and get you soaking wet, before putting it in and giving you a right good pumping." It would appear that love is not so much a smoke made with the fume of sighs, but instead – under 120 characters, and rationed out as not to incur additional phone charges. Eyes, look your last! O serpent heart hid within this Nokia 3210, why must this be transmitted to me? Technology is such a beautiful tyrant – oh, I am fortune's fool to be born into this modern age, with such aging horny relatives. Why cannot they kiss by the book?

What was I to do? "A plague on both you and your missus" I thought, putting me in this position. Do I reply back straight away or give it some time? There is the possibility that I could reply to him and he's sat at home with his tadge in his mitt, after all, these violent delights have violent ends, and he could be sat home "bashing the bishop" right now.

What should be a holy shrine of mediocrity and inane communication leaves me blushing. Regardless, I reply: "Hi uncle [name redacted]. Thank you for the kind offer. However, I will have to decline as I think it would be in breach of the uncle/nephew agreement." To which he quickly and succinctly text back, "sorry, Ads."

Under loves heavy burden do I sink. Love is heavy and light, bright and dark, hot and cold, sick and healthy, asleep and awake – its everything except what it is. And it's this; sometimes fucking horrible. Our mate, Bill Shakespeare wrote, "If love be rough with you, be rough with love. Prick love for pricking and you beat love down." But never mind love, I have to beat this memory down every time it pops into my head. O teach me how I should forget to think, thus with these texts I die a little inside.

We have now come to the end of my little tale. Good night, good night! Parting is such sweet sorrow, That I shall say good night till it be morrow, and if you are planning on sending any kind of right juicy communication, whether it be an email or text, or whatever – go wisely and slowly, as those who rush stumble and fall.

in requesting this, I am to play the honourable villain when I say, do the right thing; all the Aaron's, Adams, Alans, and Andrews have had enough, change their names in your address book, and let the Barrys, Billys, and Brians take the heat for a while.

For never was a story of more woe than me being mistaken for my uncle's hoe.

THE LORD RETURNS

It was just another ordinary day; the world was turning as it always did, people got up and went to work or school as they always did, none of the trains arrived on time… as they always did.

Then a blinding light engulfed the entire planet – most thought it was the end of the world. But when the light subsided, it was him – Jesus Christ had returned.

Everyone on Earth with a 4G signal stood still, while isolated tribes in the Amazon jungle, and people in betting shops, didn't give a shit. Every TV channel and website redirected to a live feed from Jerusalem.

As Jesus walked the streets, scores of grown men and women pushed children out the way, desperate to get a selfie with our Lord and Saviour upon his miraculous return,

Having yet not uttered a word, news broadcasters filled up dead-air with inane chatter of how "we hope to hear from Jesus any time now."

However, it started to get a bit unruly; the sheer anticipation of what Jesus had to say proving too much for some, and when it looked as though it was about to get really out of hand, Jesus addressed the crowd – "I will be brief. My message to you, my children – you must love and cherish one another, as you truly are brothers and sisters. Seek to condemn war, hate, and pollution of this Earth to the history books and commit to making a heaven of your own creation, here and now, in your lifetime. But most importantly – to the white van drivers of the world, INDICATE! INDICATE! INDICATE, YOU BUNCH OF INCONSIDERATE ARSEHOLES!"

And like that, the blinding light that signalled Jesus's arrival had also marked his departure back to heaven, and where he had stood briefly, only a moment earlier, sat a stone tablet, with the following lines inscribed in Aramaic.

Translated, it read – "MUST DO BETTER. SEE YOU IN TWO THOUSAND YEARS. LATERS KIDS. #DISAPPOINTED."

Thanks for reading!

Follow me on Twitter:

@MrAdamMcNelis

POWER ON!

Printed in Great Britain
by Amazon

79628624R00062